For Fitzy,
who was with me
every step of the way
(literally)

CHAPTER 1

THE PLAN

1. Go to NYC! For the first time in my life!
   (Aside from the 72 hours I lived there
   after traveling down the birth canal
   — TMI? probably — and being born, but I
   was 0–72 hours old, so I don't remember
   much. Correction: I don't remember
   anything.)
2. To Tisch photography camp! Yes!
   Because even though Ben Bastard (a.k.a.
   Ben Baxter) came first place at Vantage
   Point this year by using my photos, I
   came second!
3. Ignore Ben Baxter because there will be
   22 other students there from the East
   Coast. And . . .

4. There will be Dylan! A.k.a. Official Boyfriend. (Or OB, as Dace is now calling him, which makes him sound like a feminine hygiene product.) Dylan's going to work for his uncle, the Manhattan-based concert merchandise mogul, and totally see the ins and outs of working in the music industry. And meet a ton of bands. Maybe even pitch his own music to a record producer? Pipe dream, probably, but then he could forget about college—what Harvard?—and move to New York, with me (if I get into Tisch for college of course, small detail). Bottom line: Dylan + me + NYC = pretty much as awesome as it gets.
5. And Dace! Who's coming along to find an agent and start her path toward becoming the next Cara Delevingne. Minus the drug scandal.
6. So, in sum: 336 Hours. 1 Big Apple. 0 Rules.

THE REVISED PLAN

1. Go to New York alone. Why? Because:
2. Dace's mom decided that the likelihood of Dace becoming the next Cara Delevingne *with* the drug scandal was possibly greater than her becoming C-Diddy without. Or that all she'd end up doing was shopping. (Likely.) And that algebra was more important than all of the above. (Debatable.) And:

3. Dylan isn't coming either. Turned out Dylan's uncle isn't going to be in NYC because he's going to be on the road managing merch sales for the Cherry Blasters. Feeling guilty, maybe, about kiboshing Dylan's NYC trip, he offered Dylan the chance to join him and the Cherry Blasters on tour. And Dylan took it. (Obvi.)

4. So now I'm going to be in New York WITHOUT my BFF or my OB. And instead:

5. Stuck in New York WITH the single person I despise most in the world: Ben Baxter.

"I have to say, for someone who hasn't stopped talking about Vantage Point and Tisch and New York for, like, *months*, you are totally missing the point right now," Dace says, winding a section of my hair around her new five-attachment curling wand. It's the kind without the clamp, which gives you great waves, only you have to wear the glove or you'll burn your fingers off, which is why Dace is curling my hair for me while I moan. It's late Saturday afternoon and we're in my room—me on my desk chair, Dace standing behind me.

"I'd like to feel sorry for you," she says, "but I don't think I need to remind you that I'm the one who's stuck in Spalding, while you're in the greatest city in the world. Even your emo boyfriend is traveling across the East Coast with one of his favorite bands.

So can I get a little pity party over here, please?" she says, making sad eyes at me in the mirror.

I laugh. "OK, OK. You have a point."

"Aaaaaand you're done. Shake it out." I flip my head over and shake my head as instructed, then flip it back again. Dace smoothes it and nods her approval just as the doorbell rings.

"It's your big night," she says excitedly.

What she means is it's my final date with Dylan pre-departure. He's planned something—no idea what. Dace thinks it includes sex. Which I've told her a billion times it doesn't, on account of my three-month rule. She thinks I'm just holding out so that she can have sex before me, since she's always claimed she'd be first, but she doesn't even have any prospects at this point. Which would be totally fine with me, because I'm in no rush. I mean, OK, I'm not exactly the poster child for virginity at this point—er, *technically*—but Dyl and I haven't actually done *it*. No Capital S sex. Yet. And I do think that's a big deal, which is why I'm determined to stick it out for three months before I turn in my official V-card. Three months *is* kind of arbitrary I suppose, but when Dylan and I finally became exclusive BF/GF, I decided on it: Three Months. It seemed like a respectable amount of time to wait—more than, say, summer vacation, but less than an entire semester of English class, which is where we seem to only read about star-crossed lovers: Catherine and Heathcliff, Lancelot and Guinevere, Romeo and Juliet. Anyway, tonight is our last night together before we're separated for two whole weeks. Parting really *is* such sweet sorrow.

I check my outfit one last time—scoop T, black crop jeggings, brown booties, brown military jacket—and dab on some lipgloss before I run downstairs to open the door. Dylan. Those green eyes. Swoon. He grins at me, then holds out a cactus—one of those ones with the round bulb on top so it kind of looks like the Space Needle. "Needs no water while you're gone." I back up so he can come inside. He kicks his snowy boots against the doorway's metal ledge—today was December's first snowfall—as I take the cactus and place it on the small table where we throw our keys.

"You look gorgeous."

"Dace did my hair," I say awkwardly.

"I wasn't looking at your hair." He grabs me by the hips and pulls me in to him. My breath catches as he leans forward, and then his lips are on mine.

"Get a room," Dace calls as she bounds down the stairs into the foyer.

We break apart, and she grabs her coat from the banister, then slips her arms in the sleeves. "My turn." She grabs my shoulders. "I am going to miss you so freaking much," she says. Dace tested out a Swearing Ban a couple of months ago, swapping the F-bomb for Fudgee-O and other ridiculous substitutions, but that failed after, like, three days. Now she's hit a middle ground, where she swears like a rebellious Sunday school teacher, saying things like "freaking," "fudge" and "shoot" about 20 times a day. I don't know which is worse.

"I'll miss you too," I say. I wrap my arms around her and squeeze tight. When we let go, I wipe a tear and she shakes her head.

"Baby." She grins. "You really broke the seal. Dr. Judy would be so proud." It's true. I never used to cry. Like, *never.* Now, I'm basically Niagara Falls. "Remember, take as *many* cabs as you possibly can. You never know when you could get the Cash Cab." She pulls on her black knee-high leather motorcycle boots, then high-fives Dylan.

"Later dude," she says, giving him a wink.

"Bye Dace," he says, then turns to me. "You ready?"

I nod. "What are we doing?"

"You'll see." We walk down the driveway, and he opens the passenger door of his dad's old beat-up navy Cadillac for me.

We both get in, and as the car comes to life the Cherry Blasters' latest single is playing on the radio.

"You cued this up," I say, giving Dylan's shoulder a shove.

He claims innocence, and this feeling washes over me, a wave of missing him *in advance* even though he's right here next to me.

A few minutes later, we're pulling into the parking lot at Hannover Park, which is the big swath of green in the middle of Spalding. There's a reflecting pool that is, in a week, maybe two, about to turn into a skating rink, a conservatory with a massive orchid collection that Dad used to love to photograph, a children's area that's actually kind of fun even if you're not a kid and, off on its own, on the side of a gentle slope that gives it a view of the whole of Spalding valley, the gazebo where Mom and Dad were married when I was one.

"I love this place," I say to Dylan as he turns off the ignition.

He nods. We get out of the car, and he grabs my hand and leads me toward a walking path.

"Come on, what are we doing?"

"You'll see soon enough!" he teases. We make our way through the snow-frosted grass, moving farther and farther away from the town. I always find it so odd how the park clears out as soon as there's the slightest chill in the air. That's when it's at its best. A scan of the snow-dusted area around us reveals a single jogger, a guy maybe Dad's age, who passes by, the crunch of snow under his sneakers and his breathing almost in time to the bass beat coming from his earbuds. I can see the gazebo's silhouette in the distance. "It's been ages since I've been up here," I say, thinking back to the last time. With Ben. We came here to shoot together. Before I found out he was a lying thief. When I thought he was into me. When I thought he was cute. Temporary insanity—the only reasonable explanation.

Then I get my first glance into the gazebo. Dozens of tiny lights flicker, like fireflies at dusk. As we get closer, I see they're tealights in old jars, large and small, scattered around a mass of blankets and pillows of different colors and sizes. There's a picnic basket in the middle. I couldn't have pinned a more romantic scene on Pinterest.

"What do you . . . who did . . . ? Did you do this?" I breathe, which is when Dylan's hand squeezes mine. He's watching me take in the scene, and I put it all together. "But . . . how?" I step into the gazebo, then realize they're those battery-operated lights.

"This is so romantic," I say, making my way through the blankets and sitting down on a red blanket I recognize from his parents' basement rec room. Dylan reaches into the basket and pulls out two glass soda bottles. The retro kind that have bottle caps on them. "Root beer or grape?" he asks.

"Grape."

He uses his jacket sleeve to twist off the cap then hands the soda to me. He does the same for his own bottle. Then he sits down beside me, pulling a navy blanket over us.

"Happy anniversary," he says and we clink bottles. Technically, yesterday was the two-month anniversary of the day we became officially boyfriend-girlfriend—the day of Vantage Point when I rushed to the hospital and we had our first kiss. But we thought it would be more special to celebrate it tonight, our last night together before we both leave Spalding tomorrow. He rearranges some blankets beside him to clear a space, then takes our bottles and places them on the gazebo ground. Then he wriggles closer to me, pulling the blankets around us, nestling us into a cocoon of blankets and comforters, and we lie down, propping up our heads on the cushions. Dylan puts his arm around me and I wriggle in closer, into the nook of his shoulder.

"It looks different from here, less *suburban*, more . . . charmed, don't you think?" he says, and I look out beyond the gazebo's edge, to the twinkling lights down below that dot the streets of Spalding Heights, where the wealthier half of Spalding lives.

"I know—it's so beautiful," I say. "It's so beautiful, and you set this up for me—it's—" And I don't know what it is, but the lights look like they're melting, there's so much moisture in my eyes, and Dylan says, "Hey, hey," in a soothing voice and I bury my face into his shoulder.

"You all right?" he asks gently.

"I'm so happy," I say, feeling silly. "I just can't believe it's only been two months—how can you get a best friend like this in just two months?"

"It's weird," Dylan says. "The two months with you feel like forever, but the two weeks we're heading into, that seems like it's going to be forever too. But in the worst possible way."

"We're both going to be busy. My mom says it'll pass by in a minute," I say.

"I hope so," Dylan says.

"For the record, I think she's full of it."

He laughs. "You hungry?"

"Yes," I say, realizing just how hungry I actually am. He sits up and reaches into the picnic basket, pulling out Halloween-sized bags of chips, chocolate, candy.

"That's not all," he says, pulling out a red Tupperware and lifting the lid. "I baked. Chocolate chip cookies. No nuts because my girlfriend does *not* like nuts in her cookies."

I sit up too and reach into the container. I hold up the cookie, inspecting it at eye level. "Hmm, perfectly round, equal proportion of chocolate chips to batter. These might look too good to taste good . . ." I say, referring to how Dylan and I first started texting each other—taking pics and documenting food.

"Definitely not. I've broken the theory with these. They definitely qualify for a Food Alert. Go on, taste it."

I take a bite and he's right. "Yum." I finish my cookie and I wipe my hands, dusting off the crumbs. Dylan laughs, then shakes out the blanket that's over us. "You got cookie crumbs in the sheets, honey," he says, mock-annoyed, like we're some married couple in a sitcom. "I'm going to have to make you sleep on the couch." He gives the blanket one more big shake, then wraps it around me, pulling me into him until we're lying down again, snuggling as close as our bodies can get to each other. He's looking up, and I tilt my face so I'm nuzzling his neck, his hair. He smells like soap. The kind of soap that smells awesome. I could smell the guy for a thousand years.

I close my eyes. "Sometimes it seems like forever ago I was stressing over my Vantage Point entry—it feels surreal that I'm finally going. I can't wait to share every minute with you. And for you to share every minute of being on tour with the Cherry Blasters with me."

Dylan's quiet for a moment. "You know, I was thinking . . ." he pauses. I can feel his heart beating.

Say you changed your mind, I plead silently. Say you'll come to New York.

"What if . . . what if we went old school? Like

Dark Ages. No texting, no calling, no FaceTime, no email."

I push myself up, away from him, so I can look in his eyes to see if he's joking. He looks back at me. Not a hint of teasing on his face.

"You're serious? What, you want to handwrite letters? Practice our cursive?"

He looks away, up at the ceiling of the gazebo, which, I guess, has just become fascinating to him. He shakes his head and looks back at me.

"It's two weeks, and it's going to go by so fast. Let's live in the moment. Soak it all up. And then come back here and tell each other everything. Face to face. Can you imagine how intense that will be? What our reunion will be like? The stories we'll have to tell each other, when we've really lived them?"

I sit up, moving farther away from him. "Are you trying to break up with me?"

Dylan bolts up. "Are you kidding me?" He grabs my shoulders. "Just the opposite. I just think . . . I don't know, I thought it would be something we'd always remember we did. I'd miss you like crazy. But I thought . . . I guess, I thought it would be really romantic." His face falls. He's serious.

I don't want to agree to it. But I nod, promising myself I'm not going to get all sappy or clingy. Dylan reaches under the corner of the blankets and pulls out a package—a large soft square, bundled up in wrapping paper that says *It's a boy!* I raise an eyebrow.

"It was this or Christmas wrap in the basement. Open it."

I tear at the paper, then unfold the blue fleece. "Your Buffalo Sabres blanket."

"I figure you can put this on your bed in your dorm and remember our first date at the Cherry Blasters show." My mind goes to that warm fall night. When I fell in love with Dylan.

"What if you meet some groupie and fall madly in love, like in *Almost Famous*?"

"I promise I'm not going to fall in love with anyone," he says, his green eyes staring into mine.

"But you, Dylan McCutter," I say, "you're the kind of guy who could break a girl's heart without even knowing."

He runs his hand over my hair, tucking a strand behind my ear. "Not yours. It's better this way. Because if I weren't going away, I'd be sitting at home, texting you every five seconds, being that super annoying boyfriend you left behind, and you'd be having fun but then you'd feel guilty, like, *Gah! I've got to text that annoying Dylan back, only I'm at this awesome party with Tavi Gevinson but I don't want him to think I'm having fun without him—*"

"You know who Tavi Gevinson is?"

"Of course. I read *Rookie* when you're not looking."

I slap him playfully on the chest. "Shut up."

He grabs my hand, keeping it on his chest. "Come here," he says, pulling me into him, and then on top of him, and we lay there for a while. I rest my head on his chest.

"Two weeks until we're reunited," Dylan says.

"Two weeks." I run my left hand up his chest, to the side of his face, his day-old stubble rough in the palm of my hand, then push myself up so I'm facing him, our faces inches apart, and press my lips to his.

CHAPTER 2

"Why are you here?" Gabrielle smoothes her long dark ponytail, though there's not actually a hair out of place. Her intonation makes it more of a statement than a question, and she peers around at all of us expectantly. Gabrielle Brady—she was one of the judges at Vantage Point. Now, we're on her turf: a small classroom—smaller even than any at Spalding—with whitewashed walls and a panel of wipeboards and a podium at the front. The room is arranged in semi-circular rows with chairs that have those little writing tablets that fold out from the side of the chair. At first I felt disappointed, thinking we'd be in some lecture hall, stadium seating for 150, like I imagined college, but actually, the close quarters feel intimate. More important. There are twenty-four chairs, but only twenty-three of us in the seats. The missing student? Ben Baxter. Dreams really *do* come true.

It's Monday morning, 9:15 a.m., the first day of Tisch Camp, and at the podium, Gabrielle's looking impossibly elegant in her black pants and a crisp white shirt, collar up. "I want to know who you are," she says, "where you're from, why you live, eat, drink and breathe photography."

Ramona leans over, her bright red curls touching my face before she whispers in my ear. "Better think of something good," she says as though it's creative writing class and I can just make something up. Ramona Haverland—that's my roommate, and she oozes confidence. I'm hoping some of it'll transfer to me while we share our closet-sized dorm room (a.k.a., the most awesome closet I've ever been in, a.k.a. "Greeneland"—Ramona's mash-up of our last names).

Gabrielle nods to a student in the first row. "Julian, why don't you stand up and start."

Julian's dressed in a skinny black suit with a skinny black tie. He's topped with messy thick black hair that looks like somebody scribbled it in with magic marker and wearing a pair of scuffed black boots that, despite how beat up they are, give him an air of careless luxury. I bite my nail, listen to his story and wonder how I could have ever come here without investing in a new wardrobe. Anyway, Julian won a photo contest when he was *nine*. Seriously—beating out a photographer whose work had appeared in *Life*.

Next to Julian is Savida, who has jet-black hair that's shaved on the sides with the rest long and gathered into a top knot, a nose ring and big black dark-rimmed glasses. Her entire person is obscured by an enormous thick black wool cardigan that, with sleeves rolled up past her elbows and hem dangling past her butt, makes her look tiny and romantic and cozy. Plus, she's wearing these awesome skinny leather pants. Leather pants! And they look fantastic on her. If I wore leather pants, I would totally be *that girl wearing the leather pants*. But Savida somehow manages to make the cardigan her showpiece and her legwear only something that she happened to throw on, that only happened to be leather.

I pull self-consciously at the hem of my Tisch sweatshirt—the one that was Dad's. My security blanket, the one that felt so cool when I'd wear it at home. But now, I'm having wardrobe remorse. Like, why would I wear a school sweatshirt to the *actual* school I'm attending?

Whatever. This isn't fashion camp, it's photo camp. I refocus on Savida, who's explaining that she took her first photograph with her dad's vintage Nikon at age three. She's a junior at the Storm King, this Hudson Valley boarding school, where she studies digital photography every afternoon.

When Izzy, this guy with porcelain skin and freckles on his nose and big round hipster glasses, goes next, Ramona snaps her fingers and leans over again. "I knew I recognized him from somewhere— he went to Oweka. Just for one summer I think," she says, debating the comment almost with herself.

"What's Oweka?" I whisper.

"Camp Oweka. This photography camp in the Adirondacks."

"You went to photography camp?" I say, and Gabrielle gives us the evil eye for talking. Way to make a stellar first impression, Pip.

Ramona goes next, sitting up tall and pulling the ends of one of the three scarves she's fastened around her neck, and I listen, in awe, as she says she's from Brooklyn. And that she's been going to Camp Oweka all summer every summer since she was seven. "I'm the youngest of eight kids—half the time my parents are calling me by the wrong name. I *guess* I can't blame them, but it still sucks. Anyway, it's hard to feel different at home. But when I'm at camp, I feel like I have my own thing."

I didn't even know there *was* a photography summer camp. Not that Mom and Dad could've really afforded to send me. But if Ramona's parents have so many kids, how can they afford to send her to camp?

"Camp Rotunda's better," Connor, this tall guy beside Izzy, says, grinning competitively.

"Yeah well, Rotunda's for snobs. They don't have worker campers like Oweka." She holds up her hands. "Surprisingly, dishpan hands make it easier to grip the camera."

"Oweka's a fantastic camp," Gabrielle says. "We have many Tisch students who work at the camp during the summer. I'm really looking forward to seeing your work," she adds, then nods at me. "Philadelphia?"

"Watch out," Connor adds, turning his attention to me as I stand. "She's got the sweatshirt." My face flushes.

"That's so if she gets lost, she can get returned," Kai, a guy sitting beside Connor, says.

"That's enough," Gabrielle says, doing that teacher-glare-thing, which makes me feel a bit better. Then she nods at me, to go next.

I decide to go with total honesty, even if it's not as impressive as everyone else's experiences. The only competition I've placed at—the only competition I've even entered—is Vantage Point. The same contest everyone else here in the room entered—and half of them won. "Hi," I start nervously, clasping my hands behind my back so I won't fidget. "I'm Pippa Greene. I go to Spalding High in, uh, Spalding. And my dad is a photographer. *Was* a photographer."

All of a sudden a roomful of faces are looking at me, like, *what do you mean*, was *a photographer?*

"He died," I clarify, and several people gasp. "No, it's fine—he died last year."

Which actually prompts *more* gasps.

"Not like that," I say. "It was fine. Well, it wasn't fine. It was awful. It kind of wrecked me. But I'm totally over it. I'm fine."

Which sounds callous. But I am not saying another thing about my dad or death or anything else and, perhaps I should just take a vow of silence for forever. And then I blink—hard—and try to smile. How to end on an up note? "He went to Tisch. And I want to too. Just like him. That's why I'm here."

Gabrielle nods, scribbles something and then looks up. "So you . . . want to be a photographer because your father was a photographer?" she asks, somehow making it sound totally simple.

"It was something special we had."

She nods again. "That's really nice, Pippa. I think a lot of the others here can probably relate—how many of your parents introduced you to photography?" More than half the students raise their hands. I know what she's trying to do, to show me that I have something in common with everyone else, to make me feel like less of a freak, but she's just basically told me I'm not special. "It's pretty common—someone has to have that camera we first pick up and try out, right?" She smiles. "Of course, I'm very sorry to hear your father passed away. And I don't mean to make light of it, but please try to keep in mind that his memory will only go so far. I see it all too often that people have ulterior motives for pursuing this path, but it's got to come from within you. You've got to make it your own. Have your own reasons for wanting to be a photographer. But not to worry that you don't yet. That's why you're here, right?"

I can feel my face burning. This could not get any worse.

"Sorry about your dad," Ramona whispers. I shake my head. But I can feel myself tearing up. Again.

Thankfully, Gabrielle turns her attention to the door at the back of the room. I pick up my pen to scribble in my notebook, just to look busy, and pray my face isn't burning up, when my pen freezes in mid-air at the sound of a familiar voice.

"Is this the photo camp?"

Because there it is. A voice I'd know anywhere. A voice I was hoping I would not hear in New York.

I had actually convinced myself he wouldn't show. I was even thinking there was a chance I had tele-kinetic tendencies and had willed him not to come, given I'd already been here for 17 hours and hadn't seen him. So much for my superpowers.

It's bad enough that I'm already feeling super stripmall in my generic look. And then Ben has to show up and prove that not *everyone* from Spalding is so generic. I take him in—head to toe—standing in the doorway. Is it possible he aged a year or two since Friday? With his fitted mustard jeans and his navy pea coat and the burnished leather satchel and his hair, that hair, the way it's cut military-short on the sides and pushed back off his forehead like he's some '50s screen idol, he looks like he belongs here, here at Tisch, here in New York. Oh god, does he have to make it so easy to despise him?

Do you, Ben Baxter?

CHAPTER 3

THE PLAN FOR DEALING WITH BEN BAXTER

1. Ignore him. No talking to him, no sitting beside him, no texting with him, no acknowledging any part of his existence. Bottom line: Dead To Me.

It had been going *so* well. At first, I dreaded we'd be on the same bus from Spalding, and I even got Mom to bring me to the bus terminal early, just so I could stand at the front of the line, get a seat near the back of the bus and set myself up with my bag beside me, headphones on, book up in front of my face—international bus language for Leave Me Alone. Not that I really thought he'd want to sit with me after the efficacy of the silent treatment I'd been dishing out to him since Vantage Point. But you just never know—being the lone two souls who know each other can make even the worst enemies become allies. And there was no way I was risking that. But then he wasn't even on the bus. I kinda assumed he'd flown to New York, or taken a helicopter, or had a private driver in a black sedan or whatever spoiled rich kids who steal other people's stuff just for kicks do to get to New York for a camp they don't even deserve to be at.

Aunt Emmy met me in New York at the Port Authority, and we took a cab to the Tisch building to get me registered. Still no Ben. Then there was a dinner for the Tisch campers at the dining hall in Graydon Hall, where we're all staying, and he wasn't there either. And I thought for sure he'd decided not to show. That he'd decided to take the $5,000 from Vantage Point and run, or had contracted temporary amnesia and altogether forgotten about Tisch Camp. We got our checks last week—so he could've faked some non-life-threatening disease, like a reaction to gluten, and bailed. It was hardly beneath him to scam the system.

"Hey Pippa," he says now, and gives me a casual little low-effort wave, where the actual hand fluttering happens down around his waist, like an afterthought. Gabrielle gives me an interested look, and I shrug, and then she kind of confers a moment with Baxter, their low tones inaudible. But apparently Baxter passed whatever test he had to with her, because he starts up our side of the room, stops beside me and, while I feel every eye in the room on me once again, asks if he can sit in the only empty seat in the room, which just happens to be beside me. I sort of shrug as I shift in my seat.

"What's my new boyfriend's name again?" Ramona whispers into my ear, loud enough for Ben to hear.

"Trust me," I say, also loud enough for Ben to hear. "You do *not* want him as a boyfriend."

"Ben, do you want to introduce yourself to the class?" Gabrielle asks.

"Ben Baxter," Ben says, holding up his hand in a second wave, this one presidential, like we've all been awaiting his arrival and now the inauguration can begin. "Sorry I'm late. I had a few things to take care of."

AS THOUGH WE CARE.

"Well, Ben Baxter," Gabrielle says, checking her list, "give us your story—why you're here and what you're hoping to get out of the next two weeks."

Ben looks around, leans back in his chair, hands behind his head, one leg crossed over the other, ankle-to-knee style. It's his casual CEO pose. Instead of looking down at his shoes, or fiddling with his camera the way others did, he makes eye contact—first with Gabrielle, then with each of us, total politician style. He says he's originally from Cheektowaga, but that he moved to Spalding this year and is completing his final year of high school. "I just decided to take up photography for some-thing to do since the school is pretty lame and doesn't have a snowboard team like my old school. So I joined the photo club and really liked it. That's it. I don't have any skill, any formal training."

I stare at him, then back at Gabrielle, my mouth agape.

Somehow he's managed to make his total lack of experience sound enviable.

"Well, I'm very impressed," Gabrielle says as she scribbles something down. "I recall your work from Vantage Point obviously, but I never would've guessed that it was your first year seriously taking photographs. Or, what, your first month? You have some really raw talent. And your honesty—it's refreshing. It just goes to show that sometimes we stumble into our calling, but we can really go a long way if we're passionate about it."

Seriously? He fails to say anything impressive at all and still he comes out on top? How does he do it every single time? Gabrielle closes her notebook. "I'm really looking forward to having you here at the camp, Benjamin." She smiles more warmly at him than she has at any of the rest of us.

"That makes two of us," Ramona says, nudging me in the ribs.

Gabrielle explains how the camp will work: a mix of in-class lectures, off-site exercises, and time spent with a mentor—someone to learn from on a one-on-one basis. The mentors are real, working New York photographers, most of them grads of the program. She rattles off a roster of names and I recognize some of them from the fashion-world reality TV shows Dace is always watching. *America's Next Top Model. Project Runway.* These are big names. At the mention of Victor Demarchelier, Ramona squeals.

"You know who that is, right?" Ramona whispers.

Son of Patrick Demarchelier. One of the greatest fashion photographers alive. Dace's favorite photographer—he's shot a ton for *Vogue*.

"Victor's so talented. You know Grace Coddington went to his opening? They're, like, besties or something. Plus, he's super cute."

The next name's Atom Lin, who was President Clinton's official state photographer back in the '90s. People *ooh* and *aah* at their favorites. And while I've heard of some of them, I realize that maybe I haven't been living, eating, drinking and breathing photography. I like it, but am I out of my league? And then all these thoughts vanish when I hear the final name.

David Westerly.

"Are you OK?" Ramona whispers, leaning into me. "Your face is all flushed."

I nod, but say nothing, and when I look up I catch Ben watching me, but I turn my attention back to Gabrielle. She explains that all the mentors' business cards are in the glass bowl she's holding and that we'll start at the end of the alphabet and work backward. More than half the class goes ahead of me, choosing a name and reading it aloud. Ramona gets Jed Franco, a food photographer. I do a head count—six people left. Six chances to get David Westerly's name. I hold my breath as some guy walks to the front. Pulls a card. Reads it aloud. "Abigail Rosen."

I exhale. Five more.

A simple business card has the ability to change my entire two weeks here in a way that I never even imagined possible. No biggie or anything. It was good enough that I got into this camp, but to actually spend the next two weeks with David? If life ever has a chance to throw me a bone, this has got to be it. I'm not asking for the world—I'm just asking to be the one in five people who gets David Westerly. If I had a one in five chance of winning the lottery I would definitely buy a ticket. I'd probably win, wouldn't I? Well, there's a one in five chance I would.

I take a deep breath, recognizing the kind of overthinking I'm doing as the start of a downward spiral into a full-blown panic attack, which thankfully gets interrupted as Gabrielle calls my name.

I walk to the front, each step feeling like I'm walking in quicksand. I breathe in and out, mentally repeating David's name. David on the in breath, and Westerly on the out breath. David. Westerly. David. Westerly. And then the glass bowl is cold on the back of my hand.

My fingers are trembling as I pull out a single card. I turn it over and focus in on the name. It starts with a D.

"What does it say?" Gabrielle prompts me.

I stare in disbelief. "Deena Simone."

"Great. You'll love her. She's one of *Seventeen*'s best photographers—been doing their fashion spreads for years. Go on and sit down. Michael Evans, you're up next."

I walk, in a daze, back to my seat and slump down. Six months ago I would've loved to get a fashion photographer. But now I don't want a fashion photographer. I don't want any photographer except David Westerly. I stare, as three more students choose names. Finally, Ben is the last one up to the front. He reaches in, pulls out the last card and reads what's on it: "David Westerly."

Of course.

"Wanna go to Brad's?" Ramona asks as we head out the front doors of the Tisch building onto Broadway. Everyone's heading to the closest dorm caf—our meal cards work at any of the cafs, but Ramona says she knows a better spot. "All the Tisch students go there," she says, and we turn left to head up the street, the Empire State Building in the distance. "And I figured you could use a break from Connor and Kai." She shakes her head. "Don't let them get to you. Being an asshole is typically a sign of insecurity."

"I guess," I say, glad to have my coat covering my Tisch sweatshirt. "But they're right—why *did* I wear this sweatshirt? My best friend is always making sure I don't do dumb stuff like this."

"Forget about it," Ramona says, looping arms with me. "I think it's retro chic. Where'd you get it anyway?"

I tell her it was Dad's, that he gave it to me when I started to get into photography and she listens and mm-hmms sympathetically. "That sucks." And then she tells me how her best friend's sister died last year and then we talk about best friends and boyfriends and she tells me that she and her boyfriend broke up in September when he went away to college. I don't want to think about Dylan and what's going to happen next year when he goes to college.

We reach the corner of Broadway and Waverly. Unlike Spalding, where most streets are four lanes—the curbside one for parking—here in New York, the streets are just one, sometimes two lanes wide, at most, and the cars seem to zip by much quicker, like we're on some sort of closed-circuit track. Every other car is a yellow cab, which makes New York feel exactly like every movie I've ever seen that's set in New York, and again, so different from Spalding, where the only time I'd ever *taken* a cab was when we went to Florida and Mom and Dad didn't want to drive to the airport, but even then we had to call the cab. It's not like we could just stand on the street and flag one down.

The light's red for us, but people step out in front of cars coming from the right anyway, hurrying across between cars. Ramona and I stay put on the curb, and I look up, still in awe at just how tall the buildings are and just how many of them there are. Wherever you're standing, you get a different view of the city.

When the light turns green, we hurry across the street. "Ooh," Ramona says, pointing to one of those vendor tables that's set up on the corner. "Let's check out the scarves." A bright rainbow of faux silk streams from a black wire rack that sits atop the table. Knockoff designer handbags hang from hooks around the outside of the table, and on top are rows of sunglasses, braided leather bracelets, silver rings and earrings.

"You need sunglasses? Sunglasses?" The guy standing behind the table says as I pick up a pair of big, black Chanel-like glasses. He's wearing one of those oversized fisherman's sweaters and holds out a blue plastic mirror with a huge crack down the middle for me to see my reflection.

Ramona wraps an orange and purple scarf around her neck, then turns to me, lips pursed. "What do you think? Those are great on you, you should get them."

"You like the scarf?" The guy says. "That and that," he points at the scarf and my sunglasses, "twenty-five dollars."

"Fifteen," Ramona says.

He shakes his head. "Twenty."

"Done. You have ten dollars?" she asks me. I pull out my wallet, feeling guilty that I'm spending part of my Vantage Point winnings on sunglasses. Even though I won $1,500 at Vantage Point I told myself I should save as much as I could for college, and that I'd only spend some of it while here if it was something quintessentially New York or photo-related and really enhanced my New York experience. Do sunglasses really count? I pull them off to inspect them.

"You *need* those sunglasses," Ramona says. "They're awesome, and whenever you wear them you'll remember you got them in New York," she adds, as though hearing my thoughts.

I hand over a tenner and pop the sunglasses back on, and then we head down Waverly to the next intersection. "There it is." Brad's is kitty-corner to us, the white square sign sticking out of the side of the building, the head of some guy—Brad, I guess?—in the middle of a roulette wheel–like black and white striped circle. We walk around to the front door. Ramona pulls it open and I follow her in. Arcade Fire's pumping through the speakers and the place is packed. "There's apparently a super-cute guy working the sandwich bar. Ooh, grab that table," she says, pointing to the last free table by the wall of windows. "What do you want?"

"Whatever you're getting," I say and she nods. I reach into my wallet to give her another ten and she heads over to join the order line.

I put my new sunglasses on the table, my coat on the back of the chair and sit down, looking around the place, taking it all in: a girl bent over a textbook, a group of four girls laughing over their sandwiches, a guy intent on his laptop screen. All students. And even though it's probably a super stressful time of year—most students are handing in their end of term projects or writing exams—there's an energy in the air, like everyone's happy about how stressed out they are, because they're creating and doing what they love. Or so I imagine.

"I got you a chicken club," Ramona says as she places a red plastic tray on our table. "And me a phone number." She holds up her phone and does a little dance on the spot. She checks over her shoulder to see if the guy's watching, then sits down, laughing. "Are you pumped about the *Seventeen* photographer?" she asks, taking a sip of her Coke.

"I guess," I say, then take a bite of sandwich.

"Why'd you want Westerly?"

I tell her about David. How he was Dad's best friend in college. How they met right here in New York, at Tisch in first year, and were friends throughout school, but then lost touch after Dad and Mom moved back to Spalding and David stayed in New York. How David's exhibit, when it came to Spalding, was the last photo exhibit—the last real event Dad and I shared together before . . . I shake off the thought. I don't want to think about Dad being dead. Being here in New York, it's a chance for me to find out more about Dad when he was alive, in his twenties, at Tisch, like I hope to be soon enough.

Ramona's listening intently while scarfing her sandwich. She wipes her mouth with a brown paper napkin and takes a long sip of her drink.

"Wow, that sucks that you didn't get him. Maybe you can trade with Ben?"

I shake my head. "Let me tell you about Ben."

CHAPTER 4

"What makes a good photographer?" Mikael Fournier asks after we get back from lunch. He was another one of the judges at Vantage Point and is going to be one of our instructors too. He's wearing black jeans and a black turtleneck that has what looks like silver reflective tape running down the sleeves.

"This," Connor says, holding up the new Nikon D7100. "It kicks serious ass."

"Does it?" Mikael challenges. "Consider this. You go to dinner at a world-famous chef's house. Say . . . Gordon Ramsay. After the meal, what do you say? You tell him he must have a great oven? Slick pots? Nice pans?"

"Not if you don't want to get kicked *out* of his crib," Julian says, snapping his fingers for effect.

"Exactly." Mikael points at him. Nods and murmurs abound.

"So is it the camera or is it the photographer? There are some days I'm tired of lugging around my Nikon 8560, as much as I love it. So I don't. But I always have a camera with me. Even if it's this." He holds up his iPhone. "And a lot of the time, you can't tell the difference." He hits a switch on the computer at the front and the projector lights up. Two images appear, side by side on the screen. "Which one did I shoot with the traditional camera?" On the left is a guy running over a bridge—maybe the Brooklyn bridge? I can't be sure. On the right are two guys playing chess on one of those stone tables in a park.

There are some shouts for right, some for left.

"I'm not going to tell you," Mikael says. "The point is this: if it's shot by a good photographer, you can't always tell."

"So . . . this was a waste of money," Ramona whispers, lightly tapping her massive camera bag on the floor with her toe. She has every kind of lens and filter imaginable in it. I feel a bit amateur. Sure, I've got two cameras—my Canon Rebel DSLR and Dad's film Nikon—but only one lens on each. I don't even bother with a camera bag.

"Tonight we'll do an experiment. You choose your camera, and we see who's the best photographer here. Three bands—mostly students who came out of Tisch—are playing a fundraising show at XYZ. This is not only a test of your skills, but it's also your first test to see how serious you really are about photography. I say this every year and no one believes me but some of you are actually here to be photographers. Some of you think you are but will soon lose interest. And some of you—about 10%—are destined to fail. That's right. One in ten. That's two of you. Look around. Two of you won't even make it to the end of the two weeks."

I wonder how you could care enough about photography to win Vantage Point and make it to Photo Camp at Tisch, only to get here and drop out, and I decide Mikael's just doing one of those things you see in college movies—that whole scare tactic to get us to freak out and pay attention.

He hands out plastic-covered press passes, and I slip my lanyard around my neck proudly. Then I realize that's kind of a dork move, take it off and slip it in my bag.

Graydon Hall is this hive of energy and activity. There's a moment around 8:00 where I'm on my bed, blue Sabres blanket wrapped around me, staring at my phone and wondering why I ever made the promise not to text Dylan during these two weeks, when this towel monster bursts through the door. It sheds approximately 57 pounds of wet terrycloth and reveals itself to be Ramona, who stares at me incredulously. "What are you doing? We have to go in 20 minutes! Get *up*!" She slams the door shut behind her, and the huge orange cutout of Greenland that Ramona made and stuck to our door disappears.

Savida comes in, looking to borrow a hairdryer, and the next knock on the door is from Julian. "Why is there a werewolf head on your door?" he asks, but before either Ramona or I can explain that it's actually supposed to be Greenland, he's moved on, wanting to know whether we want to do a shot of Jäger in his room and Ramona quells that one: "No time!"

Which is pretty much the exact point I realize I haven't given any thought to what I'm going to wear. On my first night out in New York City.

What do people wear in New York City?

"Well, what are your options?" Ramona asks.

"Did I say that out loud?"

"What out loud? You were staring into the closet. Which is what people do when they can't figure out what to wear."

Ramona styles me: tights under my wrinkled black dress, which looks too plain and conservative until Ramona hands me her black leather jacket with about a million zippered pockets and a scarf, and then I pull on my distressed black leather Frye ankle boots that thankfully make every outfit look punk rock. I hand Ramona a stack of my bangles to complete her outfit. And then Ramona pulls me toward the elevator and Julian and Savida both end up in there with us, and then we're dashing out to the sidewalk to meet Tilly and Todd—two seniors who've been put in charge of us for the week. They're rounding everyone up and ushering them into cabs, and a minute later we're piling into one.

XYZ is this huge warehouse on the Hudson River where tons of bands have played, and there's a lineup of people at least a hundred long waiting to get inside by the time our cab pulls up to the curb outside the club. "How are we ever going to get in?" Savida asks and I giggle. "Media passes, silly," I say, twirling the red lanyard around my finger as we hurry across the parking lot.

I pull my camera out of my bag and snap a few pics of the lineup, then hurry to catch up to my new friends. Ramona and Julian are up ahead, Savida and me following, and it feels like everybody in the line is not-so-silently hating us. Then there's a split-second of panic, like what if our passes don't work, but Ramona goes first, stands on tiptoe to shout into the ear of the 'roided up Mr. Universe moonlighting as a bouncer, and he glances at her pass and nods. And we're in.

We pass through a main entrance where another round of security guards pat us down and make us open our bags. We stand in the line for coat check and then we're through another set of black metal doors and inside the venue. The place is colossal, with ceilings that shoot up into darkness, far past the rafters that have bright neon tube lights— orange and green and red and blue—running across them, like huge Star Wars–esque light sabers. Disco balls drop from intersecting rafters every few feet. Music pumps from the 20-foot speakers that line the walls—the first band's already playing up on a stage that's as deep as it is wide, with blood-red velvet curtains framing the opening, giving it a strangely intimate feeling given that there's got to be at least three hundred people packed inside. Ramona grabs my hand and I grab Savida's and Savida grabs Julian's and we snake our way through the crowd until we're at the bar.

It's too loud to ask her what she's doing, so

instead I snap some pics of the bar, and then the glasses on the bar, and then there's a glass with some sort of yellowish drink really close to my lens and I lower my camera and Ramona is pushing the glass into my face.

"Drink this!" she screams. I take a sip and realize it's definitely not soda. Red Bull, I think, plus something else. Vodka? Rum? Who knows. It's sweet and goes down easy. Too easy, I think as Savida whoops, laughs, downs her drink and disappears into the crowd. Ramona slams her drink back on the counter and holds up two fingers.

I snap more photos of our drinks, of Ramona, a few selfies of Ramona and me, and then lean over to get closer to Ramona's ear. "We should go shoot the band," I say, but she shakes her head and points at the stage. "The band disappeared!"

She laughs and hands me another drink. "Drink up!"

CHAPTER 5

Everything's foggy, like I'm looking at my room through a plastic shower curtain. I sit up, but it feels as if an elastic band is pulling my head back to the pillow. I squeeze my eyes shut, open them and focus on the clock beside my bed. Which says 8:20. At night? No, that can't be right. We didn't get to the concert until after 8:20 last night. Ohhhhhhh . . .

The concert.

Ten minutes to get to class.

I yelp, then sit straight up. "Ramona! Get up. We're gonna be late!"

Ramona moans and rolls over. I throw my pillow at her head. She swats at it, then sits up, and I can't help but crack up. Her curls stick out from her head like an orange tumbleweed. Plus, her eye makeup's gone burglar mask.

"You should see yourself."

Ramona glances at the clock. "You're one to talk."

I stand up and instantly feel like I'm on a gravity ride at the amusement park—the kind that spins you around, pushing you back into the padded wall. Sitting down feels slightly better. "Ten minutes!" Ramona reminds me and I'm back up and wearing the same clothes I wore last night. I look in the mirror.

"Let's just go," I say, and Ramona moans but puts her shoes on. A look in the mirror convinces me to pull an oversized knit hat over my matted hair. Ramona stuffs her curls under a wool cap. I grab a tissue to swipe under my eyes where my mascara's smeared and snatch my keys and bag off the desk. It's heavy—at least I didn't lose my camera last night. Ramona follows me out of the room, slamming the door behind her, and we race down the hall to the elevator.

"Come on come on come on," I encourage it. Finally the doors open and we push our way into the empty car.

Out onto West 3rd, we race up Thompson into Washington Square Park to the fountain in the middle, and then I yell, "Which way?" because yesterday we went the wrong way and so I'm not sure if left was wrong or right, but she points right and we run out through the park and down whatever street that is till the very end, which is Broadway, with the big Superdry store across the street and the American Apparel a few doors down from that, and I remember this is where we turn left, and then the building's smack there, and then we're back in an elevator, heading up to the eighth floor and flying down the hall to class. Ramona throws open the door and two dozen sets of eyes—including Mikael's—are suddenly on us as we stop, surveying the room. There are only two seats left—one on the right of the semicircle, at the front next to the instructor's podium, and one on the left, in the middle. Ramona tilts her head to the right, bugging her eyes out at me, indicating she'll take the front-row hotspot, which I'm sure she thinks is the nice thing to do because she's got to edge past six more seats than me, but the empty chair she's left me with is actually worse: it's beside Ben. I keep my eyes on the ground, and then in one continuous motion lift the writing tablet, slide into the seat, lower the writing tablet and drop my bag to the floor.

And then Ben is putting one of two Styrofoam cups that were on his writing tablet onto mine, as Mikael clears his throat and continues talking, as though we haven't totally interrupted the class.

"Drink it," Ben whispers.

I shake my head vehemently.

"It's coffee," he adds.

I lean over and take a whiff.

"Trust me, you'll feel better. I saw you last night. Figured you'd need it."

Mikael claps his hands. "All right. Let's see what you've got."

"Shit," Ramona mouths at me from across the room. "I forgot my camera."

I'm glad I remembered mine, but when I press Play to see what my shots are like, I feel sicker than I already feel, if that's possible.

The first few pics aren't terrible. For the lineup of show-goers outside the building, I employed the rule of thirds, my practiced technique. Inside, I captured the setting: the red velvet drapes that framed the stage, the disco ball hanging from the center of the ceiling, streams of glittery light on the walls. But then what comes next is just plain awful: Ramona and Savida at the bar, the bartender, pics of our drinks, pics of our empty glasses, more glasses— full, empty, full, empty—selfies where we're only half in the frame, and then a bunch of blurry photos of the band. I don't even know which band it is, the pics are so fuzzy. I remember bumping up the ISO to 1600, opening up my aperture and lowering my shutter speed to compensate for the poor lighting, but I would've had to hold my camera dead still to ensure I got blur-free photos. Or better yet, had a GorillaPod tripod, which I do have. Only it's lost, somewhere, in Greeneland.

Now I vaguely remember seeing the headlining band play, dancing with Ramona, laughing and having so much fun, but taking pictures? That doesn't ring a bell.

"I can always tell the ones who had a good time." Mikael looks around the room. "Ramona, why don't you go first?"

Ramona lifts her head from her arms, where she's been resting them on top of the desk, shakes her head, sort of grunts out something incomprehensible, then slumps back down again. I quickly pop the memory card out of my camera and am about to tuck it in my bag, out of sight, so I can fib that I left it back at the dorm in my computer, after a morning of editing, but I'm not quick enough.

"Pippa? I'll take that." He strides forward until he's standing in front of me, on the other side of my desk, hand outstretched.

I hand him the memory card. He walks briskly back to the front, pops the memory card in the computer and projects it onto the main screen. I grimace and shut my eyes.

"So you did make it there," Mikael says, and I open my eyes again. "Anything from say, inside?" He clicks through the images.

"I forgot my tripod," I offer up.

"Clearly," Mikael says. The snickers from around the room make it 10 times worse.

"I know it's not my best work," I mumble.

He nods and pops the card out of the machine, then tosses the memory card in the air. I reach out for it, but it doesn't quite make it to me, and Ben reaches out and grabs it and passes it to me. My face is burning. I want to disappear.

"Oh, I just love this assignment," Mikael is saying. "Do it every year. You work so hard to get here, and then bam, you're in New York, it's so exciting, no parents, no rules, no curfew, and you forget why you're here—or how to take a photograph that's in focus. Or some of you do. The ones who aren't cut out for this. The ones who are too interested in partying to remember to actually do their job. Do you want to be a photographer? Or do you just want to have a good time? How many of you have anything usable for your end of week assignment?" He reminds us that everything we shoot this week should be working toward an ongoing week one assignment, which we're to hand in on Friday end of day. It needs to be some sort of series, with a theme.

"You don't know that she wasn't working on that assignment. Maybe her theme is drinking her way through camp," Connor says, then flashes me a competitive grin.

Great. So now I'm pegged as the flaky party girl? How did this even happen?

"What were those—Vod-Bombs?" Ben whispers.

I don't know. I'm not *that* girl. I don't even know my alcohols.

At Spalding, I was so serious about my photography. Starting the photography club, being one of the best in the school. Everyone looked up to me. But here, I'm not like everyone else. I didn't go to any fancy camps. And now I'm the joke of the class. I'm that 10% they've already pegged to drop out before the two weeks are up.

"I really don't feel well," I say for the billionth time from under the Sabres blanket on my bed, but Ramona isn't having anything to do with my excuses.

"You didn't come here to hide out in Greeneland. I got just as shitty photos last night, and you don't see me crying about it. It's one night. Big deal."

"You didn't get publicly shamed. And Mikael doesn't know your photos suck."

"Excuse me? You totally outed me. Your pics

may have been blurry, but it was clearly me in those first drunken ones. At least there was no real proof you were drunk."

"Sorry about that," I say sincerely.

She shrugs. "Oh, it's fine." Ramona puts on bright red matte lipstick. "Hang on, I just have to run to the bathroom and then let's go?"

I shake my head. "I told you, I'm not going." There's no way I'm going to the gala tonight. I don't care if we're supposed to find and meet our mentors. Isn't that why they gave us the business cards—so we could just call or text our mentors to meet up?

I thought I'd feel better as the day wore on, but I just feel worse and worse.

I look at the photo of Dad on the desk beside my bed. Mom cut it from a scrap of leftover wallpaper from my room. For my 16th birthday, Dad gave me wallpaper he'd made out of photographs—some of him, some of my mom, some of me, some of all three of us, mostly ones he'd taken but a few Mom took or I took. Mom said she had a bit of leftover in the basement, which she had framed then tucked in my suitcase so I'd find it when I unpacked. The photo is the one of him when he was 19, maybe 20, in New York, outside his apartment on Christopher Street, where he lived when he was only a few years older than me, going to Tisch. On his way to becoming a real photographer.

What would he think of me? Working so hard to get here and then throwing it all away.

"I'm sorry," I whisper to him, hoping I'll think of something that'll make me feel better. But all I can think of is how I thought this camp would get me one step closer to getting into Tisch for college. That I'd make this stellar impression and then when I applied the admissions committee would remember me—remember hearing about me from the instructors here. How getting to Tisch Camp would give me an advantage over everyone else who hadn't gone.

Now all I can think of is the opposite. How everyone who *didn't* make it is better off. Because people like Jeffrey and Gemma, back at Spalding in Photo Club, who didn't make it here still have a chance to make a first impression on their applications. To think about what to submit, and to send in their very best, calculated work.

But me? I've made my first impression: that I care more about Vod-Bombs, or whatever I was supposedly drinking, than photography.

I lie back on my bed and stare at the ceiling—someone's taped a movie poster of *The Shining* up there. Ramona bursts back into our room.

"OK, here it is," she says. "Yes, you tanked last night. And in the eyes of Mikael, you're not exactly the star student. But you know what you are? The underdog. Under the radar. You can only go up. You can't fall from his high esteem, you don't have to worry about buckling under the pressure. You just have to do a little better each day, and before you know it, there's a chance you're the surprise hit of the camp. The most improved student. The diamond in the rough. And I'm going to make it my mission to make sure that happens. Because while I didn't IV those drinks into you, I was a very bad influence.

And I'm sorry." She swings my legs over the edge of the bed and sits down on the bed beside me.

I sit up and turn to face her. She's wearing bright pink tights and a red dress, a scarf wrapped around her wrist. Her hair's piled up on top of her head in an elastic, the curls tamed and then wild.

"That was a pretty inspiring talk."

"I do all my best thinking in the bathroom. Now put this on." She hands me a red lipstick. "Everyone will be here any minute," she adds as there's a knock at the door.

Apparently, Ramona's made Greeneland the meeting point and within a few minutes our room is packed and Ramona's standing on top of her desk, waving a purple sock and ordering everyone to file out of the room to the elevator.

The gala's being held on the Lower East Side and we make our way there, winding through a bunch of streets. Tilly's leading the pack, Todd's at the back and Ramona and I are walking together in the middle, though she's practically skipping along, talking a mile a minute—and I'm half listening, half tuning her out as I take in the streets around me. We make our way down Broadway through SoHo, past Bloomingdale's and Topshop and past a store called OMG that we think is hilarious, and then start zigzagging along Spring, with its little patisseries and cafes, to Bowery, down to Delancey past some sort of Spanish temple and finally, a few streets later, ending up on a street called Clinton.

The entrance is through the back, and we push through a set of ceiling-to-floor black curtains into a holding area, where everyone sort of disperses. We hand our coats to the coat-check guys, and then I sling my camera over my shoulder, Ramona links arms with me and we pass through another set of black curtains into a bright white space. White high-top tables are collected in the center of the room and photographs line the white walls. The lights drift from blue to purple to green to red and back to blue again. Ramona heads straight for the center of the room and aims her camera up at the ceiling to capture the balloons of colored light.

The space is packed—there have to be at least two hundred people here already, and I don't see anyone from class. "Should we walk around and look at the photos?" I suggest.

"Yes, exactly. That's exactly what we should do," she concedes, and we walk to the closest image on the wall: a sea of black hats, all tilted in slightly different directions. The inscription reads *Orthodox Jewish funeral*.

"Uplifting," she jokes, and we move on to the next photo. "How are we supposed to find our mentors in this crowd?"

"We're supposed to be learning how to network, I guess." I Googled Deena Simone and saved to my phone what seemed like the most recent photo, but who knows if she looks like what Google coughed up. But the bigger challenge is that I keep getting distracted by possible David Westerly sightings.

Someone taps on a microphone and I look around, then see an Italian guy with dark curly hair, maybe early twenties. The photographer. The reason we're here. He starts talking, thanking everyone for coming, thanking the school for the support, then talking about the inspiration behind his photos.

I try to picture myself, in five years, graduated from Tisch. Will this be me? Will I have an exhibit like this? Will hundreds of people turn up to see my work? Only if I stop getting drunk and actually start being a real photographer, I think glumly. I pull up the photo of Deena Simone on my phone again, study it, then look around the crowd.

And there he is.

He's tall, maybe six-three, and he's wearing a fisherman's cap, a caramel sweater over a blue button-down shirt, dark jeans shoved into the tops of chestnut leather ankle boots.

I pull my camera up to my face so I can watch him without looking like a stalker. He surveys the room, then approaches a woman with short platinum hair and deliberately black roots, kisses her on the cheek and nods. They talk, he laughs, crosses his arms over his chest. Then Ben moves into the frame. They shake hands, David slaps Ben on the back. Ugh.

"Come on," I say, grabbing Ramona's hand. "Let's find our mentors."

"I'd rather find cute guys to make out with," she says, and I can't help thinking that she and Dace would get along. Am I always drawn to the boy-crazy girls? But Ramona follows me around the room, and then a few minutes later, she's yelling in my ear and I turn around and she's off, standing with a man—brown sweater with elbow patches, skinny jeans rolled at the cuff, black leather boots—I'm guessing it's her mentor, the food photographer. I look around and a few minutes later she grabs my arm and pulls me over to a group of Tisch campers. We join the discussion of who's found their mentors, who hasn't, and whether we can split once we've met up with them. Julian brings up some party his boyfriend's cousin who goes to NYU is having on the Lower East Side, and Savida and Izzy are into it.

"Let's do it," Ramona says to me. Except I haven't met my mentor and I tell her to go ahead without me. So Ramona hugs me and then they split and I look down at that photo of Deena Simone on my phone for what seems like the billionth time and when I look up, he's standing in front of me. David Westerly.

His smile softens his face, which is bearded with a few days' worth of stubble in that I-couldn't-really-be-bothered-to-shave way, though I wonder if it's a calculated look. Even though he and Dad were best friends and in the same year at Tisch, he seems younger by about five years, at least. My dad had a bit of an upstate New York thickness to him, the kind people get in the suburbs from driving everywhere. David is lean, just like New Yorkers are in movies and TV shows. I resist the urge to yank at a hangnail.

"Pippa Greene?" David asks.

I nod. My lens cap chooses that moment to tumble to the concrete floor and I bend down for it, grab the thin plastic disc and am back on my way up toward vertical when the back of my head hits something hard. I clutch my head—it really does hurt—and David's grasping his chin and wincing. "Wow," he says. "*Wow*, that hurts."

I'm not bleeding, but my face is hot, and I know it has to be bright red.

"Well, Pippa, you're hard-headed like your mom, I'll give you that." David flashes a cool smile. "I'm David."

I nod. "I know." We cycle through the pleasantries, and he tells me he was friends with Mom and Dad. "I'm sorry," he adds, and I nod again.

"How is Holly, anyway?" he asks. "Still as beautiful as ever?"

I go through a couple of platitudes, that she's fine, she's great, of course she's beautiful and hilarious and mostly that's all true, if I were talking about the Mom she was before Dad died. But he doesn't need to know she's not *quite* the same ever since. He doesn't need to know she's not the same Holly she was when he knew her—when she was a real model. When she was living in New York, right after high school. That's how she met Dad. But then she got pregnant with me and gave up modeling and New York and her dreams, and they moved back to Spalding, where she was from, right after I was born.

"You inherited her beauty," he says.

"I don't know about that," I say, thinking how I'm the modified, unglam, unmodel version of her. "I think I got my dad's genes."

David raises his eyebrows. "Well, if you got into this program, you definitely inherited someone's photography skills, that's for sure—how old are you now, anyway?" He shakes his head at my answer. "Sixteen?" he says. "*Jesus*. Sixteen. It's been that long."

"I really wanted to come over and talk to you. To say hi." My voice wavers.

"Yeah, well I was about to split but I figured I better find you, so we're set for tomorrow. How do you feel about chilling at my studio? I've got a shoot at 1:30. Or 2."

I shake my head. "No, sorry, you're working with someone else—Ben Baxter."

"No, I'm *your* mentor." He grins.

"You're . . . you're my mentor?"

He nods. "Yep. We hang out. You idolize me. That sort of thing. So how well do you know the city?"

"First-timer." David's my mentor?

"Well, we'll get you up to speed in no time. I'll come get you then, and we'll walk back to my studio. It's not far."

I nod, dumbfounded. I know I should tell him again that he's supposed to be with Ben, not me. But I don't want to pass up this chance to spend the next two weeks with him. He takes his phone out of his pocket, then punches a couple of buttons. "What's your number? In case anything comes up."

I tell him and he punches the number in. He's a lefty, like me.

"Great. I'll text you tomorrow and we can figure out where to meet. Cool?"

I shake my head. "As much as I want to be paired with you, I'm not. Ben Baxter is. You were talking to him earlier. Tall guy, short sandy-blond hair? Blue sweater? What some people might call good looking?"

David nods. "Oh yeah, Ben. He's gonna hang with my friend Deena. Deena Simone. I introduced the two of them. So it looks like it's you and me, kid."

CHAPTER 6

Approximately 13 seconds of dead air happens between me telling Mom that David Westerly's my mentor and the point where she actually says something.

"Hello?" I pull my phone away from my ear. Yep, still connected. I lay back on my bed, dressed in striped leggings and a sweater dress. It's not even seven o'clock but I wanted to catch Mom before she headed to work.

Mom clears her throat. "I thought you got the woman from *Seventeen*."

"I did, but I don't know, I guess there was a mix-up."

How, exactly, *did* I end up with David Westerly? No clue. I can't imagine Deena Simone would initiate the swap. And David certainly didn't. Which leaves the only really plausible explanation that

Ben was behind the switch. But why on earth would Ben ask David? He would *never* do something as selfless as trade mentors with me so that I could get the one photographer I would die to get paired with. And how did he even know I *wanted* to be paired with David?

"Look, just be careful, OK? David . . . Well, just be careful," Mom repeats, her voice filled with worry. "Are you sure you want to work with him?"

"Am I sure that I want to learn from Dad's best friend from college? The guy who knew Dad when he lived here? Who's probably the most super-talented photographer I've ever met?" I say, then feel a stab of guilt like I'm betraying Dad in that category, but I'm making a point. "Um, yeah, like 100% sure."

A pause.

"Well, that's great news," she says, sounding like I just told her I killed all the dogs at Furry Friendz with a machine gun and the cats are next on my hit list.

"Why don't you sound happier? You do like him, don't you?"

"Of course I like him," she says unconvincingly, but she doesn't expand. She's good like that—she never blatantly badmouths something important to me. But I just don't get her reaction.

"It's not David," she fills the silence. "I'm just worried about you. You focused your entire entry to win Vantage Point around your father, and now you're going to spend all your time with David, probably asking him about your dad. What if it's too much?"

"The instructors say the opposite, actually. How important it is to embrace too much. To fully immerse ourselves. To go with something we're passionate about and follow through with it. To be a specialist, not a generalist."

"Well, OK. This is a case of Mom Doesn't Know Best then," she says wearily. "Listen, I'm just tired. And I trust you. And love you. But know that if it gets to be too much, I'm always a phone call away. And if not me, Dr. Judy."

Ramona catches my attention, pointing at her wrist, where a watch would be, but instead is just a stash of bracelets. I tell Mom I have to go, grab my bag and head out the door.

"Come on. You're hanging out with your dead dad's best friend. It's a reminder to her that her husband died and his best friend didn't. This isn't about you, it's about her," Ramona says as we walk to school. "So had you met this dude before?"

I shake my head from behind my camera, as I stop to take a picture of the roasted nuts in the food cart on the corner. "My dad hadn't seen him in years."

"What about the funeral?"

"He sent flowers."

"That's a pretty shitty friend," she says. "For the record, I've only known you three days and I'd go to your funeral. But I guess I get it. He's that way-back friend you lose touch with when your lives go in separate directions."

"Yeah," I say, but when I think of Dace, it doesn't make sense. We're way-back friends, but I can't imagine us never seeing each other again. How do you go from seeing someone every day to never seeing them again? "I guess the distance . . . they just lost touch after a while. I think Dad felt a bit intimidated by him—that he was still a working photographer in New York."

Ramona clucks her tongue. "That's what happens when you move to the burbs. That's why you can never leave New York."

There's nothing I want more than to stay in New York once I graduate from Tisch. Of course, that means getting *in* to Tisch after high school. Small detail.

Ramona holds the door open and I pass through, into the atrium. The elevator doors are just opening and we rush to fit in behind a bunch of other students.

One of whom is Ben Baxter. He looks up from his phone as the doors close behind us.

"Hi," I say, and he nods. I'm about to ask about the David-Deena swap when the elevator doors open again and everyone pushes out.

Mikael is standing at the front of our classroom, wearing a cowl-neck brown sweater with elbow patches, dark jeans, brown leather shoes. He starts by reminding us he's had more photos published in *National Geographic* than any other living photographer. He actually says it again: "I would like to remind you I've had more photos published in *National Geographic* than any living photographer. And there's a classic *National Geographic* shot I'm seeking from you: the bird's-eye view of the city. That's your assignment. Give me something *National Geographic* worthy. Work alone, work together—I don't care. But show me your best shot in three hours. Three hours. Go."

We all file back outside—everyone is chattering about what to do, making alliances, trying to keep their idea of how to get the shot secret from everyone else.

"Gareth and Belinda are heading to the top of the new World Trade Center," Ramona whispers.

"What about the Empire State Building?" I suggest.

"Ooh just like in *Gossip Girl*?" Savida says. "Can I join you two?" She pulls her thick black hair into a loopy knot on top of her head. Since yesterday she's bleached a strip of her hair blonde, only her hair's so dark it's actually kind of brassy orange, making a skunk-like stripe. She's got on huge black hoop earrings, which might actually be made of plastic, and on anyone else would look ridiculously juvenile.

Ramona mumbles that the Empire State Building's a tourist trap and probably has an hours-long wait already but I just shush her. "Can we take a cab?" I say, remembering my promise to Dace.

"Sure." Ramona sticks her arm out and a cab coming up the far lane swerves across three lanes and we all pile in. Ramona tells the guy where to go, but no lights flash, the way they do when you're actually in the Cash Cab. The cabbie zips across West 4th and then up Lafayette to 4th and then we're at Union Square and headed up Park Avenue. I snap pics along the way, when we're stopped in traffic—a set of store window mannequins in Santa suits, trees wrapped with a million little white lights, sidewalks bustling with holiday shoppers—it's beginning to look at a lot like Christmas, just like the song says. The cabbie cuts across 35th, down 5th to 34th and drops us at the corner. We all chip in a few dollar bills and then pile out of the cab and weave through the tourists and guys wearing those sandwich boards you see in movies and holding sticks with posters attached to the top advertising tours of the city, and through the main doors, following the signs to the ticket booth on the second floor. When we reach the start of the roped-off lines that wind to the ticket booth, the sign attached to the first post tells us the wait is more than five hours long.

"Five hours?" Savida says. "That's crazy. We have, like, two and a half to get the shot and get back," Savida says. "Let's get out of here. There's gotta be somewhere else quicker we can shoot." Ramona agrees and looks at me. I'm disappointed but I snap a pic of the winding line and follow them back out the way we came.

"What now?" I say as we reach the corner, and I walk straight into none other than Ben Baxter.

His head's down, he's staring at his phone but he looks up, and then when he realizes it's me, looks flustered.

"If you're planning to go up there, forget it," I say glumly to Ben.

He looks up at the building, as though he has no clue where he is. "Oh, thanks."

"Are you even doing the assignment?" I say, and he nods, but not convincingly, and then sticks his phone in his pocket. I give him a suspicious look.

"Well, no, not really."

"What are you doing up here then?"

"I just . . ." He's at a loss for words. Why is he acting so sketchy?

I look back at Savida and Ramona, who are deep in conversation and pull him aside. "You've got to pull it together. You bullshitted your way into this program but you can't just *not* do the work now."

"Ben, you want to come with us?" Ramona calls over. I exhale loudly, but Ramona gives me a *be nice* look and I feel guilty for not wanting him along. I guess it would suck if I were trying to tackle this project alone.

"So you were going to shoot from up there?" Ben asks.

"Don't get all judgy. Did you have a better idea?" I say.

"Yes," he says. "At least, more original." He pauses. "Don't give me that skeptical look. Just trust me."

"Ha!" I stick my arm out to hail a cab. Because either way, we need to go *somewhere*. Yellow cabs zip by, one after another. "Is there a trick to this?" I ask Ramona and she pushes past me, sticks out her arm, and the very next cab cuts into the lane closest to us and stops. Ben holds the back door open and Savida climbs in, but Ramona grabs the front seat, forcing me to go next, with Ben beside me for the ride.

"Where to?" the cabbie asks.

"How do you feel about wearing maids' outfits?" Ben says as the cabbie pulls away from the curb. I look at him sideways. He's looking forward, his jaw jutting out in that Abercrombie way.

"We're not shooting porn," I warn.

"I know. But trust me. This'll get us points for originality and ingenuity." He leans forward into the microphone attached to the glass separating us from the driver and Ramona. "What's the tallest hotel in the city?"

"The Diamond," the cabbie says.

Ben knocks on the glass. "OK, take us there."

A few minutes later he's pulling over to the side of the road, and we pile out onto the sidewalk. Ben pulls us aside, out of the way of the crowds, and tells us the plan. Then Savida goes into the hotel first, as directed, and we follow Ben, through the revolving doors. Savida's standing at the concierge desk, flipping her long hair over her shoulder and laughing. We walk briskly past the bank of elevators for guests while the concierge is distracted, and through a set of double swinging doors that reads *STAFF ONLY*.

There's a service elevator to the left and Ben hits the down button. "If anyone stops us, Ramona, you act like you have to pee and can't hold it a second more."

"Got it," she says. The doors open. Ben presses B for basement and holds the Door Close button. When the doors reopen, he tells us to hold the door as he rushes out, down the concrete hall to the right, disappearing from sight.

The elevator starts to buzz and Ramona takes her finger off the Door Open button, just until the buzzing stops, and then she slams her finger back on the button again and the doors open. We breathe a synchronized sigh of relief just as the buzzer goes again, and Ramona repeats the cycle. That goes on three more times before the buzzer starts a long, continuous buzz and the doors start to close on their own and there's no stopping them. I'm just about to suggest we get off because if the elevator goes back up to the main floor with Ben stuck in the basement what are we going to do, when Ben rushes through the small space in the doors, pushing a room service cart. The doors close behind him. "All right," he says, reaching under the cart and pulling out a white coat. He whips off his coat, stows it under the cart and pulls the coat over his clothes. The name on the pocket says *Javier*.

Ben reaches under the cart again, then shoves a handful of gold uniforms at us. "Put these on," he says, and I stare at him. "Quick!" Ramona tears off her coat and then she's yanking off her black sweater so she's standing in the elevator in just her hot pink bra and jeans, like she does this every day.

"I'm not stripping in front of you," I say, and Ben turns around surprisingly obediently. "Throw your stuff under the cart." I strip down to my underwear, and I focus on getting the uniform on as quickly as possible, but I've only got the maid uniform over my head when the elevator jerks to a stop and I can hear the doors opening and I'm seriously freaking out and trying to squirm into the uniform when Ben says "Sorry! All full!" and then the doors are closing, thank God, and I've got the uniform on and I step back into my boots, which looks ridiculous, but I don't have any choice. Seconds later, the doors open on the 89th floor. Ben pushes the cart out into the hallway, and we follow, Ramona asking, "Is it at all suspicious that there's a room service guy pushing an empty tray and two maids with no cleaning supplies?"

"You have a better idea?" Ben asks just as a door to our left opens. A couple—in their late twenties, maybe early thirties—walks out. She has long, straight blonde hair and is wearing a fur vest over her outfit, stretchy black pants and boots. She's complaining about how stuffy the air is in the hall, and he's ignoring her, engrossed in his phone.

"Good afternoon. We're just training the new maid staff. Do you mind if we pop into your room for a moment?" Ben asks, while Ramona and I stare.

The guy looks up at us, disinterested, and stops the door with his foot. The girl doesn't even pause, walking ahead toward the elevator.

Ben holds open the door and we walk—quickly—into the room. The door closes and Ramona squeals.

"How did you even manage that? It didn't even make *sense*," she says.

Ben shrugs, like no big deal, then looks at me. "Well, I'm sure *you're* not surprised I just pulled off a mildly petty crime with ease." He pulls out his phone. "I'll let Savida know where we are."

The room feels as big as a house—and where we're standing is just the entranceway. There's a bathroom to our right, and then a hallway so long it's like a fashion runway in front of us, which Ramona races down, and I follow, passing doors on either side. I open one, and it's a huge walk-in closet. Another goes into a dining room—a marble-topped table so long it looks like it belongs in a boardroom. There's a Jacuzzi tub in the living room and a big-screen TV that looks bigger than the screen at Spalding Screens—the old theater that plays only retro movies like *The Outsiders* and *The Goonies*. Another set of double doors opens into a bedroom so big that the king bed in the middle, complete with mahogany spires at each corner, looks like a doll's bed. Ramona rushes in and throws herself on the bed, and Savida, who found the room a minute ago, follows suit. There's another bathroom, the Jacuzzi tub reflected in a full-length mirror.

The windows are floor to ceiling, wall to wall and I walk to the edge, remembering the assignment. The view from the 89th floor is even more stunning than I could've imagined. Even though there are a few taller buildings—the tip of the Empire State Building is still visible off in the distance—we feel high. We've definitely got the bird's-eye view of this town.

Ben stands beside me. "Wow."

I grab my camera, only then realizing that the windows don't open. Which makes sense, I suppose, when you're up this high, but that means our photos will reflect the inside of the room on the windowpane. I walk into the bedroom, where Savida and Ramona are behind the drapey floor-length curtains.

"Do those windows open?" I ask. Ramona emerges, shaking her head. I check my watch. We don't really have time to try somewhere else, not if we're going to meet the deadline, and since I've already been late for class *and* handed in crap photos once this week, I'm not about to do both again.

"You think there's a rooftop we can sneak onto?" Savida says, straightening the curtains. She heads out of the bedroom. "I'm going to go look at the escape route on the back of the door," she calls, but a second later, she's back in the bedroom. "There's a maid cart right outside the door," she whispers. "We're screwed."

"How much time till we have to be back?" Ramona asks. Ben checks his watch.

"Twenty minutes."

"Maybe when we tell Mikael *how* we got these photos, from this high, he won't care that there's a little reflection," I say hopefully but I know we can't hand in photos with glare. I pull my GorillaPod tripod—Found! Underneath my dorm bed—out of my bag and mount the camera on it. All I can hope is that if I can slow down the shutter speed and keep my camera steady, you won't be able to see the reflection. I focus in on the streets below, attempting to capture a grid-like photo, but the angle makes the photo even worse than shooting with the lens right up against the glass. In the end, the only way to minimize the glare is to shoot straight out through the window, which means my shot suffers. Big time.

"We should go," Ben says eventually, putting his camera away. Savida holds up her hand, snapping a few final shots, then concedes. Ramona finished shooting a while ago and has been sitting on the couch, flipping through one of those hotel magazines with glossy photos of gorgeous hotels around the world.

"Let's lose the outfits," she says, tossing the

magazine back on the coffee table and standing. She grabs our stuff and we swap back into our clothes and stash our disguises, leaving the cart in the room, and Ben opens the door, looks both ways, then waves us out into the hall. The maid cart is outside the next room down the hall, but the maids are nowhere to be seen and we hurry to the elevator. A few seconds later we're in the elevator and riding down, acting as normal as we can when the doors open—three times—letting other guests into the car. Once we're back on the sidewalk, Ramona and Savida walk together up ahead, leaving me to walk with Ben.

"Thanks, I think," I say. "If it were up to the three of us, we'd still be standing in line at the Empire State Building to get a shot five billion people get a year."

He shrugs. "I guess my penchant for breaking the rules comes in handy occasionally."

"I think it probably always comes in handy *for you*. You just didn't bank on it benefiting me," I say, raising my eyebrows and making it come out more bitterly than I really feel, just to remind him—and myself—how much I detest him.

"Come on, at least you can crack a smile," he says, then holds the door open to Tisch. "After you."

I'm glad he's behind me, so he doesn't notice that I do smile, just a bit.

"I commend your creativity in getting this shot," Mikael says as the four of us present our photos. We chose four different views from the room, and even though mine definitely has the least amount of reflection, it's not great. "But the reflection? Kind of amateur."

"We didn't know the windows wouldn't open," I say defensively, but trying to keep my voice even.

"You didn't realize that a window on the 89th floor of a building wouldn't open? How many windows on the 89th floor have you opened?"

"None," I mumble, not adding that the tallest building I've even been in is the government building in Spalding where you get your learner's permit—and that was only 10 stories.

"Anyone know how they could've got around the glare?"

Connor pipes up. Of course. "Use a polarizing lens."

Mikael points at him. "Exactly."

Use a polarizing lens? I don't have *a polarizing lens.* "Do you have one?" I ask Ramona. She makes a face. "You'd think, given how heavy my camera bag is. Why *don't* I have a polarizing lens?"

"Any other solutions?"

Rachel, a girl who, up until this point in the camp, has been pretty quiet, raises her hand. "Widen the aperture and blur out the reflections."

Mikael nods. "Precisely. Mess with the depth of field. Not ideal, but"—he turns to look at the shot, Ben's, still projected on the screen—"better than that. All right. Who's next?" Mikael says.

The next group—Julian and Izzy and Avery—show their images, all taken mere inches off the pavement. "We shot Washington Square Park through the eyes of the pigeons," Julian says.

"It's ingenious, if not exactly *National Geographic* worthy." Mikael grins.

Ramona groans. "Why didn't we think of *that*?"

CHAPTER 7

David said he'd meet me outside the front doors to Tisch at 1 on Wednesday afternoon, but it's already a quarter after and he's not here. I'm feeling a bit like a kid whose mom forgot the after-school pickup. Ramona's mentor was waiting across the street after class. Ramona saw him, turned, blew me a kiss and rushed across the street to meet him. Yeah, Ramona's mentor was *early*. Why did I give David my phone number without getting his? I check my phone for a text from him, but there's none. Then I go to text Dace, but I know what she'll say: What are you doing on your phone? That's what you do when you're bored in Spalding, not in New York Frickin' City. And she's right. It's the whole reason Dylan and I agreed to the text ban for two weeks—so we could be In The Moment. Though I have to say I really wish I were talking to Dylan right now.

The sidewalk down Broadway's like a real-life fashion runway, where even regular people, out on their lunch break, look glamorous, just because they're In.New.York. I pull my dad's Nikon out of my bag and hold it up to my face, taking in the scene, but not actually shooting. I scan the sidewalk, left to right, through the lens, but no David. Then I see a guy across the street, standing at what looks like a hot dog stand and so I cross Waverly. But once I'm behind him, he turns, and it's not David at all. He moves away.

The guy working the stand is wearing a Santa hat and studying me. I'm about to order a hot dog when I realize it's not a hot dog stand—it's advertising something else, but I'm hungry for lunch and I figure, why not? Live a little.

"Could I have a halal, please?" I ask, hoping I'm saying it right, and the guy just stares at me. Maybe he doesn't speak English? "*Some* halal?" I say louder, pointing to the sign above his head, which says, obviously, *Halal*.

The vendor adjusts his cap. "Lady," he says in perfect English, "halal is the way the food is prepared. You're gonna have to be a bit more specific."

My cheeks go Santa red and I stare at the ground, but when I look up again he's extending a paper bag. "Try these," he says, his face softening. "First time in New York?"

"Yeah," I say, hating that it's so obvious, but I take the bag. It has three little toasty-looking balls, one of which I take out. He mimes putting it in his mouth, and I shrug, hearing Dace telling me to live a little and resisting the urge to snap a Food Alert to send to Dylan. I take a bite. The exterior is crunchy. Inside is warm, no, steamy and the crunch mixes with the spice. It might just be that I'm famished, but it tastes Food Alert–level good.

"It's falafel," the vendor says as I push the other half in my mouth. I've had falafel before, but I guess the frozen Costco version isn't exactly authentic.

"You're here for the school?" He inclines his head toward the Tisch building.

Mouth full, I nod. "Photography camp," I manage, pulling my film Nikon out of my bag for effect.

"You checked out the Walker Evans exhibit yet? At MoMA?" When I shake my head, he adds, "Great series of American cultural artifacts. Been to the PS1 yet?"

I shake my head again.

"Offshoot of MoMA. In Long Island. Great showing from Edward Burtynsky right now."

"Oh! I know Burtynsky," I say, excitedly. Recycling yards, quarries, oil spills—his specialty is industrial landscapes, but displayed on massive canvases. "He's wonderful." Except wonderful isn't the right word. "Or wonderful and disturbing at once?" I can't believe I'm having a discussion about photography with a falafel dude.

"Attraction and repulsion," he says, as a voice behind me says, "Mukhtar Abboud."

The vendor points and grins. "David Westerly." I turn.

"Pippa, I see you've met the go-to guy for the best falafel in the city."

"The young lady's experienced them," Mukhtar says, nodding at me. I reach into my bag to pull out my wallet, but he holds up a hand. "On me."

"All right, you ready?" David says, as though he's not 25 minutes late. He's carrying a white paper coffee cup and looks completely relaxed.

He downs the rest of his coffee and throws the cup in the garbage at the side of Mukhtar's stand. "Greene, let's see this," David says, grabbing my camera.

"It was my dad's."

"I know. This thing is ancient. Wow, it brings back memories." He turns it over in his hand. "What this camera's seen . . ." He hands it back. I slip the strap around my neck. "So, first things first. Coffee." He points us down Mercer. "Tell me you drink coffee."

"Of course," I say, not very convincingly. Didn't he *just* finish a coffee?

"Ah, you don't. I'll change that," he says. "I was the same way at your age. Don't worry, I'm going to tell you the two secret ingredients. First, think."

"OK . . ."

"No, Think. That's the name of the coffee house." He points to a sign a few feet away. "A lot of Tisch kids hang out here," he says as we walk up the steps. He holds open the door and I walk in. Alt-J's playing on the speakers and the place is packed with students at small, rough wood tables. We walk to the counter and he turns to me. "And the second ingredient. Chocolate. A beginner like you needs to order the mocha. Basically like having hot chocolate. Good intro to coffee. Right, Jaz?" He winks at the girl behind the counter. I look away, embarrassed for him—is he *flirting*? And isn't he a little old to be flirting with a girl who looks like she's only a few years older than me? He pulls out his wallet, and I reach into my bag, but he shakes his head. "I got it. You want to grab us lids?" He nods to a counter behind us.

"All right," he says a minute later, handing me my cup, then stirring more sugar into his coffee. There's a heart on top of mine, in the foam. "Take a sip. You don't like it, you can get something else." I snap a pic, then taste it.

"You're right—it's kind of like hot chocolate." I don't say that regular hot chocolate tastes better.

"See, you can trust me," he says once we're back outside. "OK, so now, we backtrack slightly and then you'll see the route to get from school to my studio is basically a straight line, straight through Washington Square Park." He takes a sip of coffee. "Let's talk cafeterias. You know the rundown?"

"There's a rundown?"

His eyes widen. "Hell yes, there is." We start walking as he gives me the scoop. "Palladium Hall Caf: East 14th between Irving Place and 3rd. In the Athletics Center, meaning it's one floor above the pool. So everything smells like chlorine—it's like the secret ingredient. So I'd say you want to avoid that place at all cost. However, you can't actually avoid the place because you're going to have to line up there on the weekend—brunch is epic despite the chlorine taste. Starts at 11 a.m. and is one of the best places in the city to get bagels and lox." He stops walking to ask me, totally seriously, "Please tell me you like bagels?"

I laugh, he's so earnest. "Yeah, actually. My dad—" I start and then stop. I thought I could just talk about Dad, just bring him up, but suddenly my eyes are stinging. I squeeze them tight to stop the black blotches that are starting to appear.

"Hey, you OK?" David asks, and I nod. I *cannot* have a panic attack in front of him. But a moment later, that panicky feeling is replaced by an overwhelming sense of sadness. I sort of nod-shake my head at once. Then take a deep breath, cold air making my nose hairs tingle.

"My dad was crazy for bagels. He discovered a factory that made wood-oven bagels for bakeries in Spalding and he pitched this whole photo feature to the paper just so he could get inside, and then he convinced them to sell him bagels. Every Sunday, he'd ride his bike there and they'd hand him a bag of fresh bagels out of the oven, and he'd bring them home and we'd have bagels for breakfast. He used to say, 'A life without bagels—'" My voice catches in my throat and I feel my eyes welling up.

"—is a life not worth living," David finishes my sentence. I take a deep breath and he looks over at me. "Shit. Sorry," he says. "Why did I even bring up bagels?"

"It's OK." I blink hard before any tears can escape. David nods his head toward a bench. We sit, and he pulls out a pack of cigarettes, takes one and then holds the pack out to me.

"No, thanks." I don't point out the obvious—that

Dad died of cancer. So, smoking? Not really my thing.

"Yeah, I quit last year—after I broke up with this girl who smoked. It was our thing. I had to quit." He sticks the cigarette in his mouth.

"The smoking or the girl?"

He pulls the cigarette out. "It was kind of one and the same thing. Bad for me. I mostly carry these around out of habit. It probably takes me a week to smoke the entire pack." Then instead of lighting it, he tosses the cigarette on the gravel and grinds it with the toe of his sneaker. I snap a pic.

"You should try just carrying around the empty package," I suggest, staring at the ground. "I read that in a book."

"Did it work?"

I shrug. "It was a novel."

"Hmm." He places the package on the bench beside him as a guy with a beard down to his chest passes by. He's pushing a cart full of clothes, yet he's shirtless *in December*. He stares at the cigarettes, eyes wide. "All yours, buddy," David says, holding the pack out to him. "I'm gonna keep the package though." He empties the remaining white sticks into the guy's rough hands, then puts the pack back in his jacket pocket.

"So, kind of crazy we ended up together, huh? That kid who swapped with you, what's his deal? Boyfriend?"

"So it *was* Ben's idea?"

"Yeah, said he wanted to do something nice for you."

He pauses as a woman passes by, pushing one

of those four-seater strollers. "So I was your first choice, huh? I have to say, I'm sort of surprised in light of what a shitty friend I was to Evan. Not even showing up to his funeral."

"You sent flowers." Why am I defending him?

Funny thing about funerals: you don't forget who did what. I think back to how Dylan came to Dad's funeral, even though he didn't know me. Even though we'd never even talked, not really. How that made me fall in love with him. How this other girl, Jesslyn, that Dace and I used to hang out with, sent me a text telling me she couldn't come because funeral homes freaked her out. Which OK I get, but still, you think *I* wanted to be there?

He guffaws. "Yeah. I sent flowers. Big shitty deal. Still, I should be apologizing that you won this great contest and then came all the way to New York and got stuck with me."

I shrug. "Actually, maybe you could help me with something?" I say, then pause. "We need some sort of theme for this week's project, and I was thinking maybe the theme could be my dad. All the stuff he liked to do, where he'd go, that sort of stuff." I wonder if this is a mistake. I think back to the first day, when Gabrielle totally brushed off my reason for wanting to be a photographer. But I have to believe she just didn't get the importance of Dad to my photography. This is more than a tribute to him, it's a connection, it's special. I can show her that, with another chance. I clear my throat. "I mean, if you have time. I know you've got your own stuff to do, and I'm interested in that, of course. You know,

Dad and I saw your exhibit at the Train Station in Spalding."

"Oh yeah? In the spring? I meant to actually show up at that, I was thinking I would've liked to have seen your mom and dad, you, but I had a conflict. That was . . . wow. That must've been pretty close to when . . ."

"Yeah, actually that was the night Dad discovered the cancer. The beginning of the end."

He shakes his head. I take a sip of my mocha and study the dimple in his chin to avoid making eye contact. Neither of us says anything for a moment. And then David slaps his knee. "You ready?" We stand and continue through the park. "The rest of the way is just as simple. Out the park, continue through on Washington Place till you get to West 4th." He nods at the lights up ahead. "It hits Christopher and you take it until you get to Hudson. My place is on the corner."

Christopher Street. Where Dad lived. I shiver and pull my hat down over my ears, but it's not the December weather that's giving me chills.

"Here we are, Greene," he says, pointing to an old warehouse with lengths of grid windows on each of the five floors. But no door? "We go around the back to get in," he says, as if sensing my confusion. I follow him around, through a gate to an industrial-looking metal door.

"I've been in this place longer than you've been alive." He enters a code, and then the door clicks and he pulls it open. "It's 1-2-3-4 in case you ever need to get in when I'm not here," he says, which feels really trusting and I wonder how many people he gives the code to and why I'd ever need to get into his building when he's not here, but I don't say anything. I just nod. "We all used to live right in our studios, until they turned them into work-only but some of us are still living here. Getting away with it. Late night shoots give you an excuse for sleeping in your studio."

I'm really here. I'm about to see how a real photographer lives and works. Not that Dad wasn't a "real" photographer, and I guess technically he did what David does—worked out of the house—but it wasn't the same. It was small-town. This is big time.

David leads me through another set of doors into a bare-bones hallway and a freight elevator—one of those ones where you have to pull the big metal door down with a big rope. I snap a few pics as the elevator rises in jerks and shudders to the top floor.

David pushes the door up, and I follow him down the cement-floored hallways to 505. He pushes open the door into a large rectangular space. An open kitchen off to the right, a big farmhouse-style table in the middle with benches on either side, and then a seating area off to the left—a couple of couches facing each other and one of those retro flying saucer-type chairs that are super comfy and super impossible to get out of once you're in. Beyond that is the shooting space: a few huge light stands with umbrellas, a tripod, ladder, stool, and metal table with a laptop set up on it. "Wow, this view," I say, walking over to the floor-to-ceiling windows that line the far wall. Even though we're not that high up, there's this unobstructed view of the city. I notice the sliding door to the balcony is open, and I stick my camera through and snap a few photos. If only we'd met our mentors in the morning before the bird's-eye-view assignment, I think, then push the thought aside. Everything will get better now that I'm with David.

I pull my camera up to my face and focus down on the corner. Christopher Street, right there. There's no escaping it. My heart pounds, and I lower my camera and back away from the window. I turn to see if David's noticed but he's in the kitchen, his back to me, putting a kettle on the stove. The door to the studio opens and a girl comes through the door. She's wearing a big gray parka with a fur-lined hood. She pulls her coat off, and underneath, she's tall and thin, in dark skinny jeans, over-the-knee black boots, a long caramel-colored cable-knit sweater that hangs to just past her hips. A beaded headband sits on top of her cropped platinum hair.

"Talia!" David calls, scooping coffee grinds into a metallic French press. He puts the scoop down and walks over to her, kisses her on the cheek, then slaps her lightly on the butt. She jumps playfully and makes an exasperated face at me, then shoves her coat at his chest. I do my best to keep a straight face. I don't know what to think.

"It's about time," the girl says. "I got here half an hour ago, but you weren't here, or answering your phone, so I went to run an errand. Didn't we say 1?"

David doesn't seem frazzled, not in the least. He shrugs. "Did we?"

She shuts the door. "Hi, I'm Talia," she says to me,

pushing up the sleeves on her sweater and sticking her hand out to shake mine. I take it and am about to respond when David interjects.

"This is my protégé, Philadelphia Greene. She's going to be the next big thing. Just you watch," David says, hanging her coat on a hook. Talia sits down on the bench beside the door to pull off her boots. "Talia's my assistant."

"Your assistant, huh?" Talia says, an edge to her tone.

David doesn't seem to notice, and he turns to me. "Number one rule: slippers." He points and I turn to see a basket by the door I hadn't noticed when we walked in.

"David's huge on slippers," Talia says. I look down at his feet to see he's already changed out of his shoes and into brown slippers. Tufts of sheepskin poke out around his ankles. "Make fun, but you try a pair and tell me it's not the most comfortable way to start work." I pull a pair out of the basket. They're white fun fur and kind of ridiculous but I slip them on anyway.

The kettle whistles in the kitchen.

"Next, I drink coffee all day so don't make any comments," he says, going to the kitchen and shutting off the burner on the stove, pouring the hot water into the French press. "You might call it an addiction but I call it necessary. As the day goes on I put more and more milk in it until it's essentially light brown milk."

"Otherwise he can't sleep," Talia interjects.

Dad was the same, I think, remembering the hospital. They didn't want to give him coffee, but he'd charm one cup out of them, except they'd only give him one sugar and one milk. He'd try to bribe the nurses for more. "You'd think I was asking for pain-killers or something," he whispered to me one time.

"Did my dad ever shoot here?" I ask, hopping up on a stool at the counter.

"Yeah, constantly—we shared the studio. He had his apartment, but half the time he'd be here late shooting and then just crash here. God, that seems like yesterday."

I try to picture Dad here, the two of us, instead of David and me.

"Your dad was way more dedicated than me. Kept me in line."

Talia's phone rings and she answers it, walking over to the studio area of the loft.

"Yeah but you're treating photography like the art it is. He barely ever did the kind of photography he was passionate about. I wish he would've stuck to photography as an art, not a paycheck," I say, then feel guilty, like I'm bad-mouthing Dad to idolize David or something. *Why?* But it's true. Weddings, corporate headshots . . . that's not why Dad became a photographer, but in the end it's what he spent 90% of his time shooting.

"Well, that's partly to do with living in New York versus a small town," David says frankly. "Artists aren't revered in the same way as they tend to be here—you've got to make a living." There's the slightest air of affectedness to his voice. But he's justified, I suppose. David pours a cup of coffee then holds the French press up to me. I shake my head.

"I wish he would've stayed in New York." I imagine my life in New York with a cool model mom and photographer dad. They'd take me to parties, and Jay-Z would probably be there. Jay-Z's at every cool New York party, isn't he? Of course, then I wouldn't have met Dylan or Dace.

"Yeah well, we all make choices. He did it for your mom. For you," David says, then claps his hands together. "All right, let's get going. Everyone should be here any minute right, Tal?"

Talia waves me over. "You can help me set up," she says, leading me into a storage closet with about a dozen massive rolls of colorful paper that can be used as backdrops. "David wants a gray seamless," she says maneuvering the gray roll of paper out from the back of the pack.

"What's the shoot?" I ask, and Talia says it's just tests for a new model that Silver Models has signed on.

I'm surprised. "I thought David just did candids," I say, remembering his exhibit. How he shoots real people, real life. In real settings.

"Yeah, well, you gotta pay the bills, right?" Talia says, tipping the seamless. I grab the end and we carry it carpet-thief-style over our shoulders and set it up against the far wall. The door opens and a petite girl with blunt blonde bangs and dark cat-eye glasses comes in. She's laden with multiple garment bags and dumps them onto the nearby chair. "Ugh. I hate winter." She blows on her hands and rubs them together.

"Hey Stel. Stella, this is Pippa. Stella's a wardrobe stylist," Talia says. "David's mentoring Pippa."

Stella raises her eyebrows, amused. "Wanna come help me lug the rest of the clothes in?"

I follow her down the hall. She asks me how I met David and I tell her about the program. "Wow, two weeks in New York when you're—what, 16?"—I nod. "That's kinda awesome." She pauses a minute as if contemplating this. "I wish I would've done that when I was your age. Then again, I had this boyfriend. I never would've left him for two weeks." I tell her about Dylan and the two-week communication ban. Her eyes grow wide. "That's . . . interesting," she says, which *does not* make me feel very positive about the ingeniousness of our idea. Outside the service elevator, a pile of black garment bags is lying on the concrete floor. "Here," Stella says, draping a bag across my outstretched arms and grabbing the last two from the floor. Back in the studio, she lays the garment bags on top of the others, and I do the same. She disappears into the storage closet, reappearing with a wardrobe rack. "You can help me organize the clothes," she says.

"Sure," I say. I've seen stylists at some of Dace's shoots, but the clothes were nothing like the ones we're pulling out of the bags and sliding onto the metal rolling clothes rack. Feathers and fur, snakeskin and crocodile leather adorn many of the items. Not exactly available at the Gap. "Where did you get all these?"

"Showrooms. Half this stuff never actually makes it to stores, and definitely not outside New York, but it's aspirational, you know? David wants to do a jungle theme."

"So cool," I say, as Stella unpacks a pair of spiky stilettos. "So you have to do this much work just for a test shoot?" Dace has done test shoots before, when she changed agencies, but they were never like this, never so elaborate.

"David takes his test shoots as seriously as his magazine spreads. He's helped a lot of girls into the business just on the quality of his test shoots. And fashion isn't even his main gig. Actually he hates it," she says as a tall, pale girl with dark red hair comes in.

"Jaaron," David says, going over to her and kissing her on both cheeks. She towers over him. He introduces Talia, then Stella, then me, and I give a small wave.

He tells Jaaron what he's thinking for her test shots and then shows her where she can change— a small, no-frills bathroom in the corner. Stella starts handing her outfits and David goes back to setting up his lighting, explaining to me why he's positioning the lights where he is. "Let's do a white-balance check," he says, handing me a white piece of paper. I stand where I think Jaaron would and hold it chest-high. He snaps a few shots and then nods.

"Do you want me to hold the bounce card?" I offer.

"No way, that's what Talia's for," he says as Talia moves into place, smacking David on the butt with the bounce card.

"Oh," I say, disappointed.

"Greene. What I want you to do is shoot along-side me. That's what you're here to do—be a photographer, right?"

I'm stunned for a split second but recover, totally stoked. "Um, yeah, that'd be awesome." My excitement overshadows any nervousness, and I grab my camera from my bag at the door. I sling the strap over my neck, slip the lens cap in my bag and stand behind David until he tells me where to go.

We shoot for a couple of hours as Jaaron cycles through Stella's wardrobe choices. The seamless changes to contrast or complement each outfit's predominant color. David's camera's hooked up so that his pictures automatically appear on the computer. When David says we're good, Talia goes over to the laptop to look at the selections and asks if I want to give her my memory card to see my shots on the screen. I do, self-consciously, and she pops it in the back of the computer, then cycles through the shots. "Not bad," she says, though I don't even know what kind of taste she has. It's a bit like when the sales girl at American Eagle Outfitters tells you the jeans you've just tried on look good on you, even though you know they're a size too small, because they're cutting off your circulation and giving you serious muffin top. Still, I'm flattered, and then Jaaron points to a few she wants Talia to clean up so she can use them in her portfolio, and that feels really good. Unbelievable, actually.

While Jaaron goes into the bathroom to change, Stella and I start putting the clothes back in her wardrobe bags, and five minutes in, when we look up, Talia and David are gone. Another 10 and the place is spotless. Stella looks at her watch. "I'm gonna go," she says. "Maybe I'll see you around?"

"Should I wait and say goodbye?" I ask. "It feels awkward to just leave."

"Yeah," Stella says. "It felt awkward the first time he did it to me, too. But you should just go—he and Talia might be hours. I'm sure he'll call you."

She doesn't expand, so I help her carry her stuff out to the elevator and down to the street, where she grabs a cab. "You need a ride anywhere?" she asks and I shake my head. She closes the door to the cab and it joins the whizzing traffic on Hudson. I've just arrived at my first stint of free time in the world's greatest city.

I wait for a break in the traffic and hurry across to the other sidewalk, then walk over to Christopher Street. There are trees planted in metal boxes along the sidewalk that look sort of like the fake trees I saw when we did the Warner Bros. studio tour in California a few years ago.

I look at the doors across the street. Three doors from the corner, and there it is.

Dad's apartment. The photograph I have of it is in black and white, and in my mind the door to Dad's apartment building was blue. I don't remember if Mom ever told me the color or I just decided that's what it was, but in front of me, it's a rusty red shade. I can see the number on the door, but I stay on my side of the street to take it all in. Four stories. Dad lived on the second floor. I snap a few pictures, lower the camera to check for traffic and cut across the street until I'm standing in front of the three steps. To the left of the door at the top of the steps, there's one of those metallic boxes that lists all the tenants' names, with a black square button beside each. I walk up the steps to get a closer look, scanning the list for Emmy's name. Emmy Masterson. But instead, my finger stops on *E. Greene.*

Evan Greene. His name is still on the buzzer.

"You beat me," a voice behind me says. I turn and smile at Aunt Emmy, who's standing at the bottom of the steps. I step down to the sidewalk, and she immediately pulls me in for a hug, squeezing me tight, then lets go and I take a step back. Even though I only see her once, maybe twice, a year when she comes to visit us, she looks so similar to Mom that it's almost like being with Mom—only a younger, cooler version. She's wearing dark jeans, black ankle boots, a camel-colored coat with a high collar, red leather gloves and she's got this gorgeous red leather bag slung over her shoulder. Even though Mom was the model, Emmy has always seemed more glam to me—I guess from living in New York? Or having the job she has, which does not involve scooping kitty litter or wearing a uniform that pluralizes a noun with a *z*. She's only a bit taller than me, but lean like Mom. Her brown hair's blow-dried straight and smooth. She reaches into her handbag and removes her keys. "Oh, I have something for you." She pulls out a change purse and hands it to me. It's all patchwork, various squares of fabric sewn together, a brass clasp at the top.

"Wow, awesome." I turn it over in my hands. There's got to be at least two dozen different patches of fabric, all different colors. Some plain, some with the signature *C*s.

Emmy's a handbag designer at Coach.

"I made it. It was a prototype we didn't end up using. Too time consuming to make. And time is money," she adds in a deep voice, I assume, imitating her boss. "So this is one of a kind."

"I love it," I tell her, running my hands over the patchwork.

"So, this is it," she says, as we walk up the steps. "I just want to change my shoes and use the bathroom, and then we can go for dinner, cool?"

I nod, then point at the buzzer. At Dad's name. "His name's still on the buzzer?"

"Oh yeah. I always forget about his name still being there. Except when I order takeout."

"Why—why *is* his name still there?"

She holds a finger to her lips. "Rent control. If you never give up your apartment, they can never increase the rent."

I stare at Dad's name, those white raised letters on the black strip of label-maker sticker, and try to imagine what it would be like if he were still here. If we were heading into his apartment, instead of Emmy's. If . . . what? Dad lived in New York, dividing his time, the way so many artists do: *Award-winning photographer Evan Greene divides his time between Spalding and New York City.*

Emmy's lived in Dad's apartment ever since he and Mom moved to Spalding, after I was born.

Emmy'd been living in New York for a year or so at that point, but in some tiny apartment in Queens with, like, 17 roommates, so she jumped at the chance to move in when Dad left the apartment.

Emmy unlocks the main door and I envision Dad doing the same. We walk down a narrow hallway, four rows of eight metal mailboxes on the left wall, and past a bright blue elevator door, which Emmy points to. There's a ragged white piece of paper, duct-taped to it. In thick black marker, it says *OUT OF SERVICE*. "The elevator used to work . . . back when your dad lived here. I think." She shakes her head and laughs, then adds, "Now it's a walk-up. Thank god I'm only on the second floor." We tramp up the stairs. Emmy pulls open the metal door, which leads into a hallway with four doors on one side and four on the other. I follow her to the end of the hall. Apartment 2D. The door's cream colored, with a peephole right below the number. Emmy releases two locks, and I take a deep breath as she pushes open the door. This is it. Where Dad lived, all those years ago.

I don't know what I'm expecting but you can see every corner of the apartment from the doorway. The kitchen to the right (which consists of a white fridge and stove and a tiny counter in between), couch and coffee table in front of us, bed beyond that in front of the window, two doors to the left—one opens into the bathroom, and the second is the closet, its open doors revealing racks of clothes, shoes at the bottom and a top shelf is filled with handbags and scarves.

As Emmy kicks off her boots, I try to envision Dad here. His shoes by the front door. His favorite

Tisch coffee mug in the kitchen. His slippers by the bed. His camera on the coffee table. I pull my camera out of my bag and set it down on the coffee table, just to bring the imaginary scene to life.

"Can I get you something to drink?" she asks, opening her fridge. I peer over the ledge, curious to see what she keeps inside. It's near empty, save for a bottle of wine, some packets of ketchup and a box of baking soda.

"Water?" she asks, grabbing two glasses from the cupboard and filling them from the tap. She hands me a glass and I take a sip, then walk over to the couch. The wall is a collage of photos and art—a painting, a poster, a photo of my grandparents, my mom and Emmy when they were just little girls. And then I see it. A New York street scene. In the distance, a woman, her silhouette.

"Your dad took that of your mom," she says, pointing at the woman in the background. "It was hanging here when I moved in. I kept it. A little piece of your mom and your dad with me here in the city." I stare at the photo, this photo of Dad's I've never seen before. One of the only. When he died, I spent hours, days, really, going through his photos. All the albums he and Mom kept, all the photos on his computer, boxes of photos from his time in New York. I practically memorized them all. But this one, a new one. I grab my camera from the table and focus in on the photo on the wall.

"You ready to go?" Emmy asks. She's changed into leopard-print ankle boots.

I nod, sling my camera over my shoulder, grab my bag and follow her out of the apartment and back down the stairs.

Aunt Emmy asks me what I want to eat as we head out of her apartment building.

"Something super New York."

"Everything is super New York," she says. "But I get it. How about sushi?" We walk down the street, through Washington Square Park and I feel proud of myself for actually knowing where we are.

We get to Sushi Q, which has only a half-dozen booths. While we wait for a table, I consider how everything seems shrunken here. And packed. Like you're always in the place to be—and so is everyone else. Five minutes later, we slide into a booth. A guy stops at our table. He's rocking the tattooed, buttoned-up, beard-boy look. He makes small talk for a few minutes, while I pretend to study my menu, and then he puts his cap on and walks past.

"Who was that?" I ask.

"Oh, I dated him a few times."

Emmy's never been married—mostly because she never has a boyfriend for longer than three months. She calls herself a seasonal dater—she gets a new boyfriend with each equinox, just like a new coat. Mom says she's a commitment-phobe—and that she always breaks up with her boyfriends first because she's afraid they're going to break up with her. But maybe Emmy just likes her independence.

Once we've ordered, Emmy asks me how the camp is going, and I tell her about Ramona and

Savida and a few other people, and then I finally work up the nerve to ask her about David. "Do you see David much?"

She takes a sip of her green tea. "Basically never."

"But it's so crazy—he was Dad's best friend and you've lived across the street from each other all these years, but you never see him?"

"That's New York."

"But what about when Mom and Dad would come to visit? Wouldn't Dad want to see David? Why wouldn't you all just hang out?" I say, thinking about how when Mom's old friends come to visit, all her friends get together. It seems . . . weird that Dad and David and Mom and Emmy didn't all hang out. But Emmy just shrugs and pops a piece of sashimi in her mouth.

"Besides, he's cute and talented." I pause, realization dawning, and I point at her. "You dated him."

She shakes her head, laughing. "No. *Never.*"

"Huh. Well then, you *should* date him."

She rolls her eyes. "I don't think so."

"Well, why not?"

"Why does it matter? Oh honey, let's talk about something else." She takes a bite of her handroll.

Mom doesn't like David, Emmy doesn't like David. It doesn't make sense. I sip my tea, debating whether to defend David or try to get to the bottom of why she doesn't like him either, but then Emmy's telling some story about when Mom and her were little girls, and I'm laughing so hard that tea starts coming out my nose. Maybe I'm being too suspicious about David. Maybe there is no story.

CHAPTER 8

When I get back to the dorm that night, Ben's waiting for the elevator, a copy of *Photography for Dummies* under his arm.

THINGS YOU MAY NOT WANT
EVERYONE AT PHOTO CAMP TO KNOW

1. That you know absolutely nothing about photography.

"You probably shouldn't flash that around," I say.

Ben's eyes are only half visible under his blue plaid driving cap. He looks down at the book. "Oh, come on, like it's going to matter." He shakes his head. "Sorry about today. Windows that open. Things you don't think about."

"Maybe things *you* don't think about, but I

should've thought of that. But anyway, it was fun. And what do you care, it's not like you want to get into Tisch anyway."

"Yeah, but isn't everyone in this thing kind of a shoo-in now?"

I look at him like he's crazy, and a group of students burst through the door of the stairwell into the lobby, laughing. I move out of the way as they head out onto the street.

I turn my attention back to Ben. "A shoo-in? Hardly."

The elevator doors open and Ben holds the door as I get in. It's just the two of us.

"What floor?" he asks.

I tell him 11. He pushes 10 too.

"So come on. Spill it," I say finally.

"Spill what?"

"The real reason you're here. You clearly don't care about photography or Tisch, so what gives?"

There's a long pause, and for a moment I think Ben's just going to totally ignore my question. But then he says, "My dad's Marvin Robertson."

I stare at him. "Should that mean something to me?"

"As in Marv & Harv Productions? Do you know the Countdown movies?"

"Everyone knows the Countdown movies," I say as the doors open onto the 10th floor.

He gets off. "Wait, your dad's *Marv*?"

He turns back to face me. "Yeah. You want to get off?" He holds his arm across the door so it won't close. I debate for a moment—there's no way I'm going into his dorm room, but I want to know the whole story—then step out into the hall.

"So your dad," I prompt him.

"Right. My dad's Marv. Harv's—well no one calls him Harv, it's Harvey—he's my uncle. My dad's brother. My grandpa started the company for them when they were kids. They took it over when they turned 18. Been making movies ever since."

"If you're trying to impress me . . ." I say, but don't finish it. Because I am kind of impressed, actually. But I'm not about to admit that to him.

"I'm not. I was just . . . trying to explain." He actually looks kind of embarrassed, and I feel bad for being so harsh.

"Well, why is your last name Baxter?"

"Baxter's my mom's last name," he says. "My mom and dad divorced when my brother and I were young, and my mom got custody and changed our last name to Baxter. My dad and her—they're not exactly friendly."

"OK . . ." I say slowly, trying to piece it together.

I realize we've been standing in front of a door for several seconds now. Ben points to the door. "This is mine." He unlocks the door and I peer in. "How'd you score a single?"

He shrugs and walks in, leaving the door open. I stay in the hall.

"You were just born lucky, I guess," I say, although I do like having a roommate. Ramona and I became friends right away, but Ben, he doesn't seem like he has that with anyone, really.

I lean back against the hallway's cinder-block

wall, then I slide down to the floor and stretch my legs out across the hallway, placing my bag beside me. Inside the room he tosses his satchel and *Dummies* book on his bed and retrieves something that clinks out of the mini-fridge. Then he's back out in the hallway. "Want one?" he asks, holding up a brown bottle.

"Can't you be kicked out for that?" The hallway's empty and quiet, even though it's not that late. Not even 10:00.

"It's root beer."

"Oh."

He cracks open the first one, hands it across the hall and I take it. A guy comes out of the room to my right.

"Excuse me," he says, stepping over me without making eye contact.

"OK, so go on," I say, once the guy's disappeared through the door to the bathroom, a few feet away. "Your dad." Ben slides down the wall opposite me till he's sitting too. I take a swig of root beer.

"I haven't seen my dad since I was nine."

"But you said you moved out of your dad's in Cheektowaga to live with your mom this year."

"A lie." He frowns, then shrugs. "Big surprise. We only moved because my stepdad took a job in Spalding. Who wants to move their senior year of high school, you know?" He fiddles with the label on his root beer bottle. "And I've wanted to live with my dad for years, but my mom won't let me. She wishes I'd just forget about my dad. And then her happy little world would be complete and she could stop having it hang over her head—that she failed at her first marriage."

I let this sink in, unsure what to say. I feel . . . *bad* for Ben. Like he's not as much of the jerk I thought he was, only a couple of months ago.

"OK, but what? You stole all the iPads because you thought you could trade them in for a bus ticket to New York? Or did you fly here?"

He shakes his head. "No. And that's not even why I took them. I always intended to return them. I just—I wanted to get caught."

"You wanted to get caught?" I say in disbelief. "What's so bad about your mom anyway?" Even though I keep thinking about how great it would be if Dad still lived in New York, I can't imagine not wanting to live with Mom just so I could live with Dad.

"Nothing. Not really. She's great. It's just . . . I miss my dad." There's silence and then he looks down at the carpet beneath us. I follow his gaze, looking at the carpet, which, at one point was probably slightly less beaten down, slightly brighter orange. Now it's dotted with stains.

Ben stretches his legs out so they're parallel to mine, the sole of his right shoe brushing mine, but I don't pull my foot away.

"That sucks."

"I thought I'd get kicked out of school, and my mom would beg my dad to get involved. Or he'd remember he had a son if I was a big enough delinquent. Cry for help and all that. Didn't work out that way."

"That's an understatement. I still can't believe you didn't get kicked out of school—or even suspended.

Not even for a day," I say, aware of just how close we are. How strangely intimate this hallway scene feels, despite the fact anyone could come out of their room at any time. That they'd literally have to step over us to get to the bathroom.

"Yeah, well, you know, lucky me," Ben says. "A 'cry for help' that backfired, I guess. Principal Forsythe decided I needed 'encouragement and support,' not to be 'alienated and neglected.' Which is why I still got to come here, too."

"If your goal was to get kicked out of school, why bother with photo club? You could've, like, sold drugs to preschoolers or something."

Two girls get off the elevator, laughing, then disappear in the opposite direction, into the first dorm room to the left of the elevator bank.

"Come on, the Vantage Point prize—cash and a trip to New York—I figured it was a pretty good way to get here. A Plan B if getting kicked out of Spalding backfired. Or vice versa. I thought taking pictures would be a cinch. I didn't realize it actually required skill. Or that you would be so good."

"Thanks . . . I guess? But did it ever occur to you that you nearly derailed my whole college plan?"

"To be honest, I really wasn't thinking about you."

We're both silent. The only sound is the whirr of the heating system through the vents that line the hallway. I watch him as he stares at his knees.

Finally, he looks up. We lock eyes. "It was really shitty. I'm sorry."

I don't say anything for a moment, but I don't break eye contact. Then I nod, look down, and when

I look back at him, he's taken off his hat and is fiddling with it. He looks pretty miserable, but I fight not to let my guard down with him.

"I just don't get it," I say, my tone a little less harsh. "Why not just come to New York and see your dad?"

"My mom would never let me. I've asked so many times before. She always said no. So I knew it had to be something school related, somehow—something that just happened to be in New York. Something she couldn't deny me. Even now she made me promise I wouldn't try to contact him."

"Really?" I can't imagine Mom not allowing me to see Dad, even if they had divorced. "So when are you seeing him?"

He lets out a sort of half-laugh. "That's the thing. I'm not. I haven't even been able to *talk* to him. And now I'm realizing I can't fake my way through the program." He tosses his hat on the ground beside him. "But if I fail out they'll let the school know and they'll tell my mom. I won't be able to stay here"—he motions to his room—"so then it's back to Spalding."

"Are you kidding me? We've been here four days already and you haven't seen him?"

"I know. I . . . I've tried calling but his assistant answers his phone, I guess. And I don't know if she's not giving him the messages or what, but he never calls me back."

"So keep calling."

"I know I should. It's just—what if . . . what if she gave him my message that I'm in New York and that's why he's not calling me back? What if he doesn't want to see me?"

"Of course he wants to see you." I try to sound certain, but I'm not. I pull my knees to my chest, hug them tight. "What ifs . . ."

"I know. What ifs are a waste of time."

"That's what I was going to say."

"That's what Dr. Judy always says."

"Dr. Judy?" I ask, feeling embarrassed. He knows I see a psychologist? I sit up straight, crossing my legs underneath me. All I can think is that he's been reading my diary. Except I don't actually keep a diary. *Dace?* Did Dace *tell* him?

"My mom made me start to see a therapist after the whole 'incident.'"

My mouth drops open. I snap it shut. "Wait. What? You see Dr. Judy? Really?"

"Yeah." He looks confused.

"I've been seeing her ever since my dad . . ." I trail off.

Neither of us says anything for a moment.

"So, bonding over shrinks," he says.

"Psychologists," we both say at the same time, then laugh. Ben holds his bottle out to cheers. I clink the glass against his.

"OK and what about her office—the empty book-shelves?" says Ben.

"I know! Like, why even have bookshelves if you're not going to put books on them?"

"She's probably a fraud."

"Takes one to know one," I say. I mean for it to come out as a joke, but it ends up sounding harsh. I cough. "Have you talked to Dr. Judy about finding your dad?"

He shakes his head. "You ever feel like when you're supposed to talk to Dr. Judy, it's actually the last possible moment you ever want to talk to her?"

"Isn't that the point?"

"Well, what would Dr. Judy say, in this case?"

"What would Dr. Judy say? Sounds like a great hotline. For when Dr. Judy's too busy."

"Playing solitaire."

"Checking her email."

"Blogging."

I take a sip of the root beer and it tastes so good. I never drink root beer. Why not? I *love* root beer. Or, is it this *conversation*? No, obviously it's the root beer.

"But seriously," I say, "she'd say that you're trying to play it all out in your head instead of letting things play out as they will. That the only action you can control is the one you take. So you should do that, don't you think?"

"You think she'd actually say that?"

"No. Not really. I think she'd say, 'What do you think I should tell you?'"

"Dead on."

"You're in New York. Your dad is famous. He's filming one of the biggest movies of the year. You have to find him. I'll help you," I say before I realize what I'm even committing to.

"Really?" he asks, looking pleasantly surprised. "I'd really owe you." And something surges inside me.

"You traded me for David Westerly, didn't you?"

He's looking at me intently. "I asked him not to tell you."

"That was a nice thing you did, Ben Baxter. But why? And how did you know I wanted him?"

"I guess I could just tell when they read out his name in class." He looks at me.

I look down at my shoes, considering my next words. "Well thanks. So let me owe you one for that."

CHAPTER 9

The rep theater is tucked away behind a strip of costume shops. "Good find, right?" David says. It's late Friday afternoon and the sun is shining but the alley is cast in shadow. I snap a few photos of the graffitied walls and the marquee sign. There's a Star Trek film playing in a little over an hour. For now, the theater still looks pretty dark. Instead of pulling open the doors, though, David snaps his fingers. "I'll show you the way your dad and I used to sneak in." He leads me back down the alley and into one of the costume shops, which reeks like sweat socks. David raises his eyebrows at me. I laugh. We walk through the racks of costumes—French maids and cowboys, Superman and orange inmate jumpsuits.

"Can I help you find anything?" an old guy calls from behind an old wooden desk.

I peer over, but David grabs my hands and pulls me behind him.

"No we're great, thanks!" says David, and then we're ducking behind a rack of clothes and he's opening a metal door and we're through it and into the theater.

The reek of sweat socks lingers, but now it's mixed with buttery popcorn.

"How did you know how to do that?"

"It's never locked," David says. We're in the lobby, to the left of the ticket booth by the entrance. "We were broke. Desperation is the mother of invention."

There's a guy sweeping the red carpet at the entrance, which seems like a pretty ineffectual act, though he's intent on his job; he barely reacts when he notices that we've appeared inside the lobby, not through the main doors. "Movie doesn't start for another hour. And there's no previews," the guy calls out, still focused on his broom.

"OK if we just sit in the theater for a few minutes? My . . . niece"—he points at me—"she's doing a school project on buildings from the '20s. We'll leave before the film starts."

He glances up, shrugs OK, and we head over to the concession stand. There's a girl loading kernels into the popcorn machine, a six-inch layer of old popcorn lining the bottom. We order snacks—popcorn for David, Twizzlers for me, which makes me think of Dylan and for a split second I desperately want to text him, but instead I tell David I'll also have a Coke, and he orders the same. The girl behind the counter fires the dark liquid from a soda fountain gun into waxed paper cups, then sets them on the counter and pushes them closer to us.

"Your dad and I would sneak in that way most times," David says as we put lids on our cups. "Well, actually, your father would want to pay—he could be so straight-laced, but sometimes I'd convince him to be a bit wild, and we'd come through that way, which is when we'd actually get popcorn with the couple of bucks we'd saved, so technically the theater was still getting the same amount of money out of us, and then we'd go up here." He motions for me to follow him up the stairs to the theater's balcony. Cradling the popcorn in his right arm, he pulls the door open with his left. "After you, Greene."

I walk into the dark theater and head straight to the front row of the balcony. I've never sat in a theater with a balcony, and it feels very regal and retro. Whenever Dylan and I have gone to the movies we usually sit on the side, so if the movie's slow we can, well, have a mini makeout session without getting heckled by the people behind us. I think back to the sci-fi movie we saw last week. Totally *not* makeout-inspiring material, but that didn't stop us. Actually, I'm not sure there is a movie we wouldn't miss part of for the chance to make out. Isn't that what Netflix is for?

We settle into our seats and I realize how tired I am. It's been a long, full day. The photography grads needed the eighth floor for the entire day so they could set up for their party tonight, so that meant an impromptu off-campus mentor day for us campers.

Totally made up for the eight-plus hours of intensive instruction we got in class yesterday, with only a break for lunch. So by 10 this morning I was heading over to David's to coerce him into spending the day showing me more of Dad's favorite haunts. For a moment I thought he was going to say he was too busy, but half an hour, two cups of black coffee and a hot shower later, he came around.

We started out sort of non-eventfully in Central Park, to check out a rock by a willow tree that Dad loved. David told me my dad went there at least once a week, and I told David how Mom and Dad were married surrounded by the willow trees of Hannover Park, and then we sat under those willows, on the rock, taking it all in—hidden, but with a view of the park. I snapped pics of the horse-drawn carriages, a guy working a cart of quintessential New York souvenirs—Statue of Liberty snow globes, I heart New York T-shirts, postcards and magnets—a group of runners, a squirrel running up a tree. It felt warm for December, or maybe New York is just warmer than Spalding, but I slipped my gloves off and into my coat pocket—it was freeing to be able to shoot with my bare hands.

Now, I look down at my hands, holding my camera, and I remember why we're here. I get up, walk over to the aisle and snap some photos of the theater, shooting down into the mezzanine from the balcony. Then I sit back down beside David.

David's quiet, watching me. He's been chatty all day, but I wonder if he's been holding back. Keeping it light on purpose, just to keep this whole day, this whole life-with-Dad-in-a-day re-enactment, from becoming too heavy. But I want more out of him.

I put my feet up on the railing. "So, yours and Dad's friendship . . . it was, pretty easy? Just good times?" I hold my breath.

"Sure, we had a lot of fun." He pops a handful of popcorn into his mouth. "It was college," he says after he's swallowed. I feel disheartened, but then he adds, "You know, I was going to drop out in third year."

"Really? Why?"

"I'd scored this internship in London, and I thought it was the coolest. I was going to take off, go there and travel around Europe, pick up girls— everyone was doing it. Sleeping in hostels, sleeping their way around Europe. Drinking their faces off. And I was cocky, tired of school, of assignments, of teachers. It all felt so . . . pedestrian. Like, was this really art? I wanted to create *art*. The internship was working alongside Gustav Lebrun. He was doing all this crazy experimental photography.

"I told your dad. We were sitting right here." He tosses another handful of popcorn in his mouth, crunches down on it. "Actually we were sitting over there," he points down below, to the main level, off to the left. "The movie was *8½*. Fellini. Subtitles. We were talking through it. Anyway, I tell him this, and he isn't supportive." He pauses, taking a sip of his drink. "He tells me, 'Stick it out. Finish what you started. Follow through.'"

"And so you stayed in New York because of what my dad said?"

Instead of answering, David grabs my camera and

hits the Play button. "Shoot this one again, Greene—
try focusing in on the railing and blur out the background. Play with your depth of field a little."

So much for a revealing conversation. There've
been glimpses of something more to Dad and his
relationship—certainly after we left Central Park,
when I convinced David to show me where Dad and
Mom met. It slipped out, actually, a comment David
made about Mom nagging them about whiling away
all their time at The Root—a pool hall they'd go to
instead of to classes. He been reluctant to take me
there, though he wouldn't say why. And when we
got there, I'd had to basically play the dead dad card
before he'd tell the story of how my parents had met.

Finally, he'd caved. "It was the fall we started
second year. We'd just gotten back into the city,
after a summer at home—him in Knoxville, me in
Philly. The Root had opened a few weeks earlier and
everyone was talking about it. We were waiting in
line—we had no clue what we were in for. And then
they lifted the metal plates up and they let three
people at a time go down. It was in the basement,
so there were these steep stairs from the sidewalk
down into it. Anyway, they'd let in three people.
Exactly three. If you were only two, they sent the
next person in line down with you. They were crazy
about that rule. There was a rumor it started as a
joke, but then they just kept at it, kinda being pricks
about it, or whatever. So we get up to the front and
we're about to go in, and the guys behind us won't
split up, and out of nowhere this girl comes up—this

vision. She's tall and willowy with flawless skin and auburn hair . . ."

"Mom?" I interrupted in mild disbelief.

He cleared his throat. "Yeah, your mom. She came up beside us and planted a kiss on your father's cheek and then . . ." He hesitated.

"What?"

"Then she plants one on my cheek too."

"Wait, you already knew her?"

"No, that's the thing," David said. "Neither of us had ever seen her before. Holly was so calm, acted like she'd just stepped out of the line to catch up with a friend or something, just waltzed ahead of, like, a hundred people in line. I bet your mom is still doing crazy stuff like that."

Mom, smooth? Skipping a line? Kissing two random guys to cut the line at a club? The only line Mom stands in now is at the grocery store. "Uh, not exactly."

"No? Well, I guess she's been dealing with a lot lately. With your dad and everything."

We sat quietly then—an obligatory moment of silence for this lost Holly go-lightly side of my mom—and then David picked the story back up.

"I guess we sort of expected her to say thanks and ditch us, but she didn't. She asked which one of us was going to buy her a drink. So I go. Grab three beers for us. And . . ."

He paused then, almost as though he'd forgotten what happened next. Or didn't want to say what happened next. Or maybe it was that he was right back in that moment, living it again. Eventually, he continued.

"... the rest is history," he finally finished simply.

"Wait, what? What *happened*?"

"Your mom didn't tell you any of this?" he asked cautiously.

"She said they met at a bar and started dating right away. That's all she ever told me."

He'd nodded. "Yeah, well that was basically it. It was clear your dad was totally into her and she was into him, and that was it. Your dad asked her for her number and they were together from then on. Two peas in a pod." He adds, an edge to his voice. Is it resentment? Or maybe jealously? But no. Dad always said David didn't want a girlfriend. Didn't want to settle down.

David stopped the story there, said he wanted a smoke—not just to hold the pack—so we left the bar and wandered a bit in silence, until he shook off whatever fog he was in and brought us here to the theater. But there was something off, something nagging at me. Mom and Dad always said they met when Dad was in his final year at Tisch; they'd dated less than a year before having me. Which doesn't mesh with David's story of meeting Mom at the start of second year. But before I could dispute it, ask David to retell the details, David was back to sharing old college tales of him and Dad—college pranks involving refrigerators, notable dares involving flagpoles.

Now, in the theater, instead of refocusing the shot the way David suggests, I bring the conversation

back to the internship. To what seems like a signifi-
cant point in their friendship. "So you didn't take
the internship. Did that fight change things between
you two?"

David puts his bag of popcorn on the ground
in front of him. "I guess, yeah. I guess it did. I
thought it was selfish of him to tell me not to do it.
I thought he was jealous that I'd gotten the internship and he hadn't." He wipes his hands on his jeans,
then crosses his arms over his chest.

"He probably knew what he was talking about.
But it was a pivotal moment in our friendship, in our
lives, that's for sure. And it happened right here."

"Do you wish you'd just ignored him? Gone to
London instead?"

"I do. You think 16 years later I'd still be in the
same studio, shooting hairspray campaigns to make
my rent?" He runs a hand through his hair.

I didn't realize he *did* shoot hairspray campaigns
to pay his rent. Just like I didn't know he did test
shoots for models just starting out. I thought . . . I
guess I thought he made his living doing the kind
of photography I saw when Dad and I went to his
exhibit at the Train Station. *Art.*

"I see now that your dad wasn't jealous about the
internship—he was looking out for me. I had this
long-term girlfriend, pretty serious actually, and
Evan was trying to encourage me to commit to her.
He was trying to get me to stay. Do the right thing.
Course at the time, I couldn't see it."

My surprise is evident in my voice. "What happened to the girl?" Did this girl break him? Is she the

reason he's never had a long-term girlfriend since? Never married? No kids?

"We broke up. I didn't go to London, and I resented her for it, I guess. So I'll never know how it would've played out . . . just proves we take our own fate in our hands in the end, right?" David stands, checks his watch. "Just about sunset. We should get to Times Square."

I stand and follow him as he heads up the aisle. That's it? That's the end of the story? So we can go to Times Square?

"Uh, does this have anything to do with my dad? Did my dad even *like* Times Square?"

"Like? The guy *loved* the place. Loved all the people, all the lights. I never understood it. Most touristy spot in the city, most *avoided* place by true New Yorkers, and Evan loved it. You can take the boy out of Knoxville, but you can't take the Knoxville out of the boy, I guess."

And so, 20 minutes later, we get off the subway at 48th and 7th. Lights everywhere. The pixelboards reach high into the sky. I've seen them on TV, when Ryan Seacrest counts down to New Year's, or in movies—but I always thought it'd be more impressive onscreen than in real life. But it's not. It's even more surreal in real life. I snap a bunch of shots, focusing in on the hundreds of tourists who are taking their own photos of the bright lights, of the sky-high buildings, of themselves.

Eventually I lower my camera and head over to David, who's sitting on a bench, waiting. He's reading a crumpled copy of the *Village Voice*. "You hungry?

It wasn't just the lights your dad loved about Times Square." He folds the paper, tucks it under his arm. Then he leads me down a side street, and we stop in front of a yellow sign with red writing that says *Phil E. Cheesesteaks.*

I can't help but laugh. "My dad was full-on addicted to cheesesteaks. I never understood it."

"Why do you think we're here, Greene?" David asks, pulling open the door. "This was his favorite spot. And they *are* the best cheesesteaks in the city. Best I've ever had, frankly. And I'm from Philadelphia, so that's saying something." I snap a bunch of photos as I enter the no-frills sandwich shop, trying to picture Dad here. Then I make my way to the counter, and we place our order with the large guy in a white cook's jacket. I get mine with extra mustard, just like Dad liked it.

CHAPTER 10

It's not the usual view of white walls when the elevator doors open onto the eighth floor of the Tisch building on Friday night. Instead, the photography floor's been transformed. On the wall, there's a huge flashing pixelboard, like a massive Lite-Brite, that says *SENSORY OVERLOAD* in a rainbow of colors. Behind that are hundreds of white balloons, floor to ceiling and wall to wall. Ramona whoops and rushes forward through the balloons. I follow her, laughing. The sign was no joke. Music pumps from hidden speakers, and cold air blasts down on us from an overhead fan that's been hitched to the ceiling with bungee cords and electrical tape. Every inch of wall is covered in photographs. But not just regular photos. These are three-dimensional tactile photos—the first one has a girl on a bed, only the bed is made of a tiny spongy mattress. A photo of 12 x 12 bottlecap tops, all different colors, has one actual bottle cap in the center. A pair of white shoelaces have been threaded through a photograph of blue and white high-top Converse on a patch of green grass.

"Check this one out," Ben yells in my ear, coming out of nowhere and pulling me over to a huge mural—a movie theater, complete with actual lit-up tiny runway lights down the aisles. It reminds me of earlier today, in the theater with David.

"What'd you do for your project?" I ask, spotting a pile of coats and adding mine.

"Project?" Ben says noncommittally. Ben's wearing navy skinny cords and a polo shirt that's hugging his biceps.

I give him a look. "The one we were supposed to be working on all week—the one that was due today at 6?"

"Oh right." He moves down to look at the next installation.

"So?"

"I didn't do it."

"You didn't?" I can't hide the surprise.

"Come on, Pippa. They expect 10% to flunk out. I'm helping them meet their expectations." He smiles at me.

"Don't be ridiculous." I swat him lightly on his upper arm. "If you just try . . . I've already had two bad assignments. Out of two. If this were baseball, I'd be batting, what? Zero? I would *definitely* be on the bench. But you gotta keep trying. What if they kick you out before the camp's up? You'll have to go home without seeing your dad."

He shrugs. "I can't do a huge project with a *theme*. I'm not cut out for this."

He starts to walk down the hall, but I grab his arm and pull him onto a nearby bench.

"You have the perfect story to tell—finding your dad, the super-famous movie producer, who just happens to be in New York at the same time as you."

He shakes his head. "There's no story if he won't call me back."

"OK, no offense but for someone who was practically running an underground electronics theft ring, you kinda suck at this. Ever heard of Twitter?" I pull out my phone, and I get a wave of homesickness— or, more accurately, Dylansickness. I know there's no reason to have any texts or missed calls from him, but still, it doesn't make it any easier to see nothing there but the picture of Dylan and me, the selfie we took our last night together, lying in the gazebo, blankets and pillows all around us.

I open my Twitter app and punch in #Countdown in the search bar, then hold my phone out for Ben to see. "I told you I'd help you, didn't I? What about tomorrow? We could find him."

"The assignment was due today, remember?"

"So we'll tell Gabrielle that you needed till Monday. That the Countdown movie wasn't filming, or something, and that you need one final shot from the movie set to complete the assignment. Surely you can think of something believable." I smile.

"I didn't think you were serious about helping me."

"It'll be '*The Amazing Race* of Marv Robertson.'"

He locks eyes with me—those blue eyes. "Really?"

"Besides," I say, looking away, trying to brush off what almost felt like a *moment*, "isn't Christian Bale in the new Countdown? Not exactly a hardship if I get to meet him."

Ramona runs over, wearing a pair of hipster glasses and waving another pair. "Put these on. There's a photobooth in the corner. We have to get our pic taken together. For prosperity." She grabs my hand and pulls me into the crowd.

CHAPTER 11

I pull the covers off Ramona's head on Saturday morning. She makes a sound like *arghinipakman*. Or maybe it's *ragabukiman*. "Nooooooo" is her first sentient word. Then: "Whyyyyyyyyy?"

"I feel the same way. But we have to help Ben with his photo project," I say.

"First, you do *not* feel the same way, or you would not be upright. And second, why do I have to? This was not *my* idea."

To be fair, she's right. It wasn't her idea and why *does* she have to help?

"Because you're my roommate?" I say meekly.

On a scale of one to ten my hangover is probably about a two, which feels like an achievement. Especially given how much everyone else was drinking. Head shake. Ouch—OK, a bit of a headache. We're not talking a rolling boil. More like a gentle simmer. Standing up produces nothing like the nausea that had me wanting to bear-hug the toilet just a couple of days before. Pasty mouth? Nope. Gritty eyes? Nada. OK. So just a headache. Which is probably mostly due to the fact that I got about four hours sleep—max. So I can deal with you, headache. Let's hang out for a while. It's *fine*.

"Remind me again?" Ramona rubs her eyes, smearing last night's makeup.

"What?"

"Why I'm helping you help Ben? This isn't about being your roommate." She rolls out of bed, squints, then looks at me, eyes wide. "You *love* him."

"Um, what?" I say. "You are clearly still drunk."

"He stole your photos and seems to be doing everything he can to sabotage his time at Tisch." Ramona whips off her T-shirt and boxer shorts, then looks around the room. She grabs a G-string, bra and tights from the top drawer of her dresser. "There's no other plausible reason you want to help him."

"So he's a bit messed up and does stupid things, but he has a good heart," I say defensively.

"Plus, he's very cute." She raises her eyebrows at me, then throws a green cable-knit sweater dress over her head.

"Is he?" I say innocently. "I hadn't noticed. Anyway, point is I don't want *him* to get the wrong idea. Which is where you come in. Group hang. It'll be more fun with you there."

"Well, there's no denying that." Ramona grins,

grabbing her fur vest off the back of her desk chair. "Fine, convinced!"

Ten minutes later we're carrying our camera stuff down the hall to the elevator. Out on Ben's floor, I'm about to knock on his door when it flies open and there he is—looking really . . . *ready.* I push away the thought that his hair, which is still wet and messy, looks anything other than messy and wet. Because this is Ben Baxter, who, up until two days ago or something, I despised more than anyone ever. I'm guessing it's my headache. And the sleep deprivation that's making me soft toward him. *Clearly.*

No one can bear the thought of the prison-food stench in the caf so we walk over to Brad's, where, over hot drinks, Ben tells us about the brainwave he had last night for his project.

"Wildlife photography!" he says. "Like a nature documentary. Except we're not shooting poisonous tree frogs or the red-tailed anteater. No—we're shooting something in his natural habitat—the Hollywood movie producer."

I feel secretly proud of Ben that he's embracing this whole situation and really trying. Like maybe my little pep talk yesterday worked. And also that he's not fully bailing on this project, which I was a bit worried about. Not because I *care*, but because Ramona would kill me if I dragged her out of bed for no reason. Obvi.

"So what's our plan for finding him?" Ramona says, resting her head on her arms, which are crossed on the table in front of her.

THE PLAN FOR FINDING BEN'S DAD

1. Right. A plan. I guess we didn't go much further than Twitter on my phone last night. Hmm.

Ben looks at me. We both look at Ramona.

"You two are hopeless." She pulls out her phone, and I can see her typing *Marv & Harv Productions*.

"How did I not know that my dad's company has an Instagram account?" Ben groans.

"A very active Instagram account that posts pictures from their movie sets," Ramona mutters. Ben and I both lean over Ramona to see her phone and I avoid noticing the smell of his—what? Aftershave? Deodorant? Conditioner? It's like juniper berries mixed with soap. Or something.

The pics give us glimpses of filming locations in the background. There's Christian Bale looking into a camera with director Jack Penn, and a couple of the other cast members playing some video game in a remote trailer. But the ones that interest us are the ones with Marv. He seems to be everywhere around these shoots.

"What Countdown are they doing, now?" Ramona asks.

Ben counts off on his fingers. "This one's the fifth."

Ramona whistles. "That's a lot of dough."

"Yeah, well," Ben says. "I'd rather have a dad I see more than . . . never."

"Is that the Williamsburg bridge in the background?" Ramona peers closer and we lean in, too.

"OK, so that puts them in Brooklyn. But north or south of the bridge?" She thinks, then nods. "It's got to be north. There's no green space south—too industrial."

"I'm so glad you're from New York," I say, jumping to my feet. I'm the first to the street and as usual the cabs pass me by until Ramona basically steps in front of one, points and shouts, "YOU." The cabbie is obedient. Piling into the back, Ramona commands the driver, "Williamsburg. North 5th and Berry." I climb in after her, then Ben pulls the door shut behind him. There's that hump in the middle, and my legs are on either side of it; my right leg is slightly resting up against Ben's, in that way that's kind of inevitable when you're the one sitting in the middle, and my leg feels tingly beneath my jeans.

Williamsburg feels like a different place from the one they show you in the movies and on TV shows. I thought we were going to see beards, glasses and jeans rolled at the ankles on every guy passing on the street in Hipsterland. And we do, but the streets themselves feel grittier, more rundown than I imagined. We get out in front of Blue Bottle Coffee and go inside to get snacks. Ben's on Instagram, I'm on Twitter. Ramona's making sure we don't get hit by cars as she leads us down a series of streets. "We've got to get to the water," she says. "They have this outdoor market at East River State Park on the weekends—Smorgasburg—and near there could be where the pics were taken." As we get away from the little down-town-ish streets with shops and cafés, the streets get dirtier, the buildings more abandoned and there are more shifty-eyed locals scurrying past us. Or maybe it's just my overactive imagination.

Eventually we get to the water, and there are the tents signaling the outdoor market and tons of people taking advantage of the sunny, not-so-cold December day, but there's no sign of any movie shoot.

"Let's keep going along the water—that way?" Ramona suggests, and we keep walking toward a narrow strip of parkland. Some guys are playing hacky sack without coats. Ben waves down a guy who's running on an asphalt path near the soccer field. The guy, still running in place, tugs on the white cord around his neck and his earphones pop out.

"Have you seen any movie trucks around here?" Ben asks.

The jogger glances over at Ramona and me, then back to Ben before he shakes his head, then pops his earphones back in and takes off. We try again with the next person who passes by—a woman pushing a baby stroller—and then the next, until finally, about seven people later, we strike gold with a guy in his mid-thirties, who nods encouragingly. "Yesterday, they were shooting at the field—right there. Everyone said it was the new Countdown movie. I saw that guy—the one who was Batman? But they're gone today."

Ben looks defeated.

Ramona checks her phone, then looks at me. "Anything?"

"Someone just tweeted at Cake Boss to ask if they're in the Countdown movie. Where's *Cake Boss* filmed?"

"At the actual bakery," Ramona says. "Carlo's Bake Shop. Over in New Jersey." Ramona looks around. "We've got to get to the PATH system." I look confused. "It's like the subway but different, and it'll take us right into Hoboken and then it's just a short walk. Cab back into the city is probably easiest." We start walking down the street, and Ramona runs ahead to the next corner, leaving Ben and me to walk side by side. Ben turns around and walks backward to check for cabs behind us, and I grab his arm just before he's about to back into a lamppost.

"Guys!" Ramona calls after she flags down a cab. Ten minutes later we're back in Manhattan, and the cabbie's pulling over at the corner of Christopher and Hudson. Is Manhattan really *this* small that all these things happen at this intersection? We follow Ramona down into the station, taking the steps two at a time, find the machines, put in our money and get a two-way card, then follow the signs for the PATH trains down another flight of stairs to the track. The train is pulling into the station, and we get on. It feels exactly like being on the regular subway, only there are no stops and everything is really dark for a really long time outside the train. We sit in a row—Ben, me, Ramona. There's a nervous energy between us. A total adventure, but none of us wants to jinx it, because it's not just for fun.

When the doors open, Ramona jumps up and Ben and I follow suit, racing up the escalator and out the terminal. There's less personality here and more plain function, I notice. Ben's camera's to his face, documenting it all, and Ramona's figuring out which way to go. "Come on," she leads us up a street I notice is also called Hudson, which is just plain confusing, like we've entered some sort of time warp and haven't crossed out of Manhattan at all. We turn onto Newark Street and see this huge lineup before we even hit the next corner.

Ramona says that's for Carlo's Bakery. "Lineup's that long all the time. It's the only real bakery in town, so if you actually need a birthday cake or, like, cookies, you have to show your address to prove you live here and don't just want a selfie to Instagram."

We walk alongside the lineup of girls and their moms and then pass the doors to Carlo's, where everyone's snapping pics in front of the sign. One of the guys from the show—I'm guessing, he's got dark hair, could be Italian and is wearing a white apron—is posing on the street with a bunch of girls our age, who are shamelessly flirting. No sign of a *Countdown* film crew anywhere.

The rest of Washington Street is quiet after that. It seems straight out of a movie, one of those made-for-TV ones that play on Sunday night. The whole street is little shops—a hardware store, a restaurant, a clothing boutique—most of their windows decorated for the holidays. We walk to the other end and back, checking side streets as we go, but there's no clues at all. Eventually we head back to the city on the train.

"This is pointless," Ben says, as we're sitting on the orange vinyl seats. The doors open and we stand up.

"It's not," Ramona says.

I check my phone as soon as we come out of

the station. There's a new photo posted on the Instagram feed—yachts moored at a harbor.

"Where's this?" I ask, holding my phone out to Ramona.

"Hard to tell, but maybe Chelsea Piers? Come on."

And then we're in another cab heading up 11th Avenue along the Hudson River, past Pier 26, zipping along the waterfront trail, past joggers and cyclists and rollerbladers, even in this weather, and then we're hopping out at a huge bright blue complex and Ramona's deciding where to go. "If we could see the yachts, then they have to be over here," she says, leading us to the north side of the buildings. There's a skate park, and green space and then, in the distance, past the tennis courts, I spot the line of white trucks, parked along the street. We race toward them, eye on the prize.

People with clipboards, headsets, walkie-talkies, cameras . . . there's no doubt this is something, but is it the Countdown movie?

"How do we find out what's going on here?" I say aloud. If it *is* a movie, is anyone involved actually going to tell us which movie?

Ramona points to a bunch of teens on the other side of the park. "That's how." She races over, and a second later, she's back, nodding. "Countdown."

"We did it!" I say excitedly. But Ben's not himself. His face is pale, and he's fidgeting.

"What do we do now?" I ask, and then I realize that's exactly what he must be thinking.

"Do you know what his assistant looks like?"

I say. He shakes his head. "What if you try calling your dad again?"

He scrolls through his phone and dials.

"Straight to voicemail," he says.

"Well, let's just start asking people. Come on," says Ramona, looking around, and I'm glad she's here to lead the charge. She nods at a cluster of women with headsets. "Let's split up. Someone's got to tell us at least if your dad's even here. Marv, right?"

Ben nods. Ramona heads to the right. I go for a guy who's winding an extension cord around his arm. I turn back—Ben's watching me. Not moving.

"Do you know where Marv Robertson is?"

The guy looks me up and down, shakes his head. I move on to the next, a girl carrying a tray of coffees. She shrugs.

A dozen more people at least, before I get to a woman coming out of a trailer. Headset on, clipboard in hand. She doesn't look up before replying.

"In a meeting."

"Where?"

"The usual."

"Can you remind me . . ." Luck runs out as she looks up.

"Who are you?"

I point back to Ben, who's somehow escaped to sit on a bench. "Me? Nobody, really. But that's Marv's son. He needs to talk to him. It's important."

"His son? Nice try."

I walk back to Ben. He looks up, a mix of hope and discouragement in his eyes.

"He's in a meeting. We just have to wait for him to get out," I say.

"What if . . ." Ben starts.

I shake my head. "No what-ifs."

Ramona comes back a second later. "Wow, his assistant's a total jerk."

"You found his assistant?"

She nods. "Marv should be out any minute."

But any minute turns into many minutes with no action. Into hours. We keep our eye on the trailer that Ramona says he's in, but there's a nervous silence among us. We're just sitting there on the bench: Ramona, then Ben, then me. Ramona starts playing Candy Crush on her phone, and I take a deep interest in photographing the individual bits of gravel at my feet, and Ben gets up and starts walking around, snapping pics here and there—it's not clear what his focus is, and he's gone awhile. Eventually when he returns to sit down with us, Ramona is the one to say what we're all thinking. Should Ben go to the trailer? Knock on the door? After a beat, he nods and stands, like a boxer in the corner of his ring. I stand behind him, like the coach, and Ramona nods that I should go with him. I don't want him to have to go through it alone. I follow him over to the other side of the park and wait at the end of the trailer as he climbs the three steps up to the door. He knocks tentatively.

Nothing.

He knocks again, then tries the handle. It's locked. The lights are out in the trailer. He turns, looks at me and makes his way down the steps till he's standing beside me.

"He must've left."

"Maybe he didn't get the message," I offer immediately, but we both know that's probably not the case at all. Ben takes a deep breath, then starts walking in the direction we came. Ramona looks at me questioningly, and I shrug.

"It sucks," I say to Ben as we follow Ramona back to 11th. He doesn't say anything, just stands solemnly as Ramona hails a cab, and we all get into the backseat.

"Where to?" the cabbie asks in a total announcer voice.

"West 3rd and Thompson," Ramona tells him, just as a rainbow of lights flash on the ceiling of the cab.

"Oh my god! Cash Cab!" I scream, pointing.

"That's right! You're in the Cash Cab!" the guy proclaims.

"What's going on?" Ben asks, totally confused.

"*Cash Cab!*" I slap his leg. "We have to answer trivia questions to win money!"

"That's right," the cabbie says, explaining the rules. "You've got 13 blocks to go. I'll ask you questions. For each question you correctly answer, you'll win $50, but as the questions increase in difficulty, so does the cash you could win. Are yoooooooooou ready?"

I have never been more ready for anything in my life.

"What do you call the unpopped kernel at the bottom of a bowl?" he asks a second later.

"Old Maid," Ben announces without hesitation.

Pause. Ramona and I stare at him, then she squeals and I clap my hands and the cabbie says, "You're riiiiight! That's $50. Next question."

"What is the only state whose name is a single syllable?"

"Maine," Ben says immediately.

"You're riiiiight! That's another $50."

"How did you know that?" I ask, shocked.

"I like geography?" he says, looking a little sheepish.

The cabbie watches us in the rearview mirror. "What's the only fruit that has seeds on the outside?"

"Strawberry," Ben says again, before Ramona or I can even think of anything. Not that I'm complaining. Ben's surprise trivia expertise may be the best secret he's ever kept.

One more question, which Ben answers without pause, and we're on to the $100 round.

"In what season do the most burglaries take place?"

We all look at each other. Ben shrugs. Ramona looks at me, wide-eyed.

"Winter?" I guess, then hold my breath. The lights flash.

"You're right!"

Ramona reaches across Ben to hug me, squeezing us all together.

And the questions keep coming. And we keep getting every single one right. Somehow our combined knowledge is unbeatable. And then the cabbie says the next question is our final one. I bite my nail.

"In what year was the first successful photo-graph taken—1808, 1827 or 1832?"

The three of us look at each other. Blankly.

"This is embarrassing," I whisper.

"Why didn't we learn this yet?" Ramona whispers frantically.

"Should we just guess?" I say. "The middle number?"

Ramona and Ben both nod. "1827," I say, not at all confidently.

Silence. Then the lights flash, all different colors, and the cabbie starts beeping his horn and cheering. He pulls over in front of our dorm. Then turns and hands us a wad of $100 bills.

Ramona grabs them and we all get out of the cab. Ramona practically clobbers us with excitement. "Guys! We just won *Cash Cab*!" She waves the money in the air. I'm too stunned to really register it. Dace is going to die.

"What should we do with the money?" Ramona asks as she doles it out—$500 for each of us, one $100 bill left over.

"Celebrate?" Ben suggests. "Let's go out. Let's *do* New York." I nod, Ramona nods and then we agree to meet back in the dorm lobby in an hour, ready for our night out together.

CHAPTER 12

"I understand you wanted to document the things your dad did or liked while he was here, but it just didn't work for me," Gabrielle says during our one-on-one on Monday. "It's not really a day in the life, and it's not a progression of any sort, really. It's just a bunch of shots of store signs, bright lights, an old movie theater. An apartment. There's no focus."

I sit in stunned silence, registering her comments, before pulling myself together, sitting up a little taller in my uncomfortable wooden chair and responding. I did *not* expect this. Not after the great weekend we had—going out Saturday night, meeting up with everyone else from the dorm to go to Brad's, which was throwing a study-break dance party, and then Sunday going to the famous brunch with everyone at Palladium Hall.

"But these are the places he'd go to 16 years ago,

and they're still around," I explain now, to Gabrielle. "So it's like Time Standing Still," I say, feeling proud of myself for coming up with that theme on the spot. "My dad died," I reiterate. Maybe she's forgotten. "You know, I didn't know about any of this, because I'd never been to New York. But my aunt, she lives in my dad's old place, and David Westerly's my mentor and he was my dad's best friend, and he showed me all the places they used to hang out. It's, like, getting to *be* with my dad, even when he's not here."

"That must've been really *nice*. Getting to see those places. I just . . . I don't think it's really telling a story. What you just told me isn't present in the images. Do you know what I mean?"

I start to nod, just to agree with her, just because I feel so uncomfortable and want to get out of the room. But then I stop myself. The way Dr. Judy's taught me. Not to panic-attack my way out of an uncomfortable situation to avoid it. I have to confront it. If being here is important to me. If photography is important to me. I sit up straighter in my seat. "I don't think you understand what I was going for. For my Vantage Point theme I shot things that reminded me of my dad and that was good enough to get me here . . ."

"Good enough." Gabrielle looks like she's eaten something terrible. "That's not really a term I like to hear. And as I recall you didn't just take a bunch of pictures of things that reminded you of your dad, you had a theme . . . what was it?"

"Darkness in Light."

She nods. "Right. So, sure, you took inspiration

from your dad, but you built a theme. *That's* what I want you to do. Explore a photography technique or an artistic idea. Take inspiration but then take an inspiring photo. Move us. See here?" She holds up the photo I took of Aunt Emmy's apartment. "A wide shot inside the apartment."

"I employed the rule of thirds," I say, pointing out how I positioned the couch in the frame so that it runs up the right third of the photo.

She nods. "Sure, but your depth of field is all off."

"Oh," I say, when what I really mean is, "Huh?" Because David mentioned that when we were in the theater too, but I was more interested in his past with Mom and Dad than I was with his photography advice.

"Where's the focal point here? You've got the couch in focus, but what about this," she points to the white envelope—the piece of mail Emmy had brought inside and stuck on the ledge inside the door, the ledge that separated the front entrance from the kitchen. "Who's it addressed to? I'm more curious about that. Who lives here? Give me something to be nosy about, show me something I couldn't otherwise see." She flips to the photo of Phil E. Cheesesteaks. "OK, so it's a sandwich shop. You've shot the sign. Have you ever looked up anything on Google Earth?"

I nod, remembering how last summer Dace and I were obsessed with Google Earth when we heard the car was coming to Spalding. We were practically on 24-hour watch for an entire week, and we had this whole plan to run outside with, like, all our clothes on—winter coats, three pairs of pants, hats, mitts, scarves, ski goggles—in the middle of one of the hottest days of the year. We thought it would be *so* hilarious. Only we never saw the car and, probably, only we would've thought it was funny.

"Well you could see *this* on Google Earth. But what about *this* guy," she says, pointing to the guy who was entering the shop as I was taking the photo. He's out of focus, but as she points closer, I see he's not wearing shoes. I didn't even notice that. "There's a story there. He's not wearing shoes in December—and he's in a sandwich shop?"

"Anyway." She checks her watch. "I've got to move on to the next student. But I will say this, Pippa. You have raw talent, for sure. But it feels like you're stuck in the past. You're seeing photography through the memory of your father, rather than through your own eyes, your own experiences. It's holding you back. I want to see what you see, I want to see *you* in your work. Otherwise, I'm not interested."

"Pippa!" Ben calls for the third time. I turn to see him dodge a car as he crosses Broadway to catch up to me. I wait at the curb.

"Hey," he says, out of breath. "Didn't you hear me calling your name?"

I shake my head even though that's not true. The snow is starting to fall, the sky dark even though it's only midday, and I pull the hood of my coat up around my face.

"Where are you going anyway?" he asks, as we walk under the scaffolding, past the American

Apparel, down Broadway. I'm purposely heading away from everything I know—the dorms, Brad's, David's loft. I don't have a plan, only to get away from it all. We're only on a lunch break, supposed to return to class in an hour, but I'm not going back.

"Hey, what's wrong?" he says, seeing my tears. I swipe at them with the back of my mitten, the fluff sticking to my lipgloss. Why did Dr. Judy have to be so damn good at her job?

"Gabrielle hated my assignment. She was going on and on about what I've done wrong, what I could do better, but I actually just . . . don't get it. I don't think I belong here."

"Hey." He tosses an arm around my shoulder, like we're friends or something, and gives me a squeeze. "Don't be ridiculous. Whose photos got me here? You have what it takes. You definitely belong here."

"I don't think I do. I don't . . ." I sniff. "I don't have the same skill level as everyone else."

He grabs my arm, and sort of twists me toward him, looking me in the eye. It feels too intimate, and I look away, but he touches my cheek with his bare hand and turns my head back to look at him. "You have the most passion for photography of anyone I've ever met. It's your *thing*. Don't let one assignment, or one teacher, get you down. You know a hell of a lot more about taking photos than I do. You know, aside from taking other people's." He smiles. "Come on, even that deserves a smile, no?"

I force a smile. His blue eyes are caring, genuine.

"Anyway, I was chasing you down because I wanted to say thank you. Gabrielle loved my assignment. And it's because of you. I never would've even thought to document the whole '*Amazing Race* of Marv Robertson.' The reason I did well on this was you. You forced me to tell the story of trying to find my dad. So thanks."

"This is turning into a pattern," I say miserably. "I fail at my own stuff, while somehow aiding and abetting so you come out on top. That's got to mean something."

"We make a great team?" Ben says, then reddens ever so slightly and coughs. "Anyway, thanks. A lot." He shoves his hands in his pockets. "Hey, what do you say we skip class this afternoon? Go see a photo exhibit at MoMA?"

Even though the thought of going to see that Walker Evans exhibit the halal guy mentioned is appealing, even though going back to class is the last thing I want to do, even though Ben wouldn't be the worst possible person I could spend the afternoon with, I shake my head. "I can't."

Ben gives me a long look, then turns and walks back toward the school. I watch him for a moment, then turn and walk, alone, in the opposite direction.

CHAPTER 13

"Cancel the shoot. With no assistant it's not only too much work, it's too much of a headache. Bunch of annoyingly chipper Britney-Spears-circa-2000 girls running around in sneakers?" David's on his phone when he throws open the door for me, finally, on the third round of knocking. It took me a good hour of wandering the city, certain I was going to get lost and trying not to care, to decide what to do. Actually, it took David's call, just when I was thinking I would go back to class after all, saying he needed help on a re-shoot and could I come over. And so I did.

"I don't care that the client wants it done. This is *not* who I am. Can't you use someone else? I'm not some chump who shoots ads. I told you that."

He makes a face at his phone and hits the red End button and tosses his phone on the big oak table where it lands with a clunk.

"Fucking rent," he says.

"Where's Talia?" I ask, dropping my bag, kicking off my shoes and slipping into my usual pair of slippers.

David shuffles over to the kitchen and pours two cups of coffee.

"It wasn't working out," he says grumpily, rubbing his eyes with his forefinger and thumb. He hands me a mug.

"The assisting or the girlfriend-ing?" I take a sip and put it down. I'm definitely not ready for straight up coffee. Not even at one in the afternoon.

"She wanted to move in. They always do. I had to cut the ties. Same story as always."

"You've broken up with her before?"

"No, not her, exactly. Assistants in the past. Always ends the same way."

My look of shock-surprise-intrigue makes him raise his hands in the air. "What? Don't get judgey. I can't help it. Hot women apply to be my assistant. I'm supposed to purposely choose a not-hot woman?"

"You don't have to have sex with them just because they're pretty."

"Yeah, yeah."

"So what was that on the phone?" I say as he sits down at his computer.

"Shoot tomorrow afternoon. A fucking sneaker campaign."

"I could help. I still have to assist on a photo shoot before the end of the week. I know I've helped you with some other stuff, but technically we're supposed to be involved in the whole thing, start to finish, not just by fluke," I add, feeling discouraged.

"We'll see. Can you put that light stand away? We need the bigger one." He nods at the stand by the seamless. I grab it with both hands and heave it over to the storage closet, then look around to figure out where to make it fit so it's not in the middle of the room. I move one of the seamlesses over to make space, but as I'm maneuvering the light stand into place, it knocks a box off the nearby shelf.

Photographs spill on the ground all around me.

"Everything OK, Greene?" David calls.

"Yes!" I call back and begin sweeping up the photos. They look old. They're dusty, with faded postcards, receipts, slips of paper and opened envelopes mixed in. I sweep the contents together. There's a great shot of the New York skyline, the rooftops in focus, the Hudson River out of focus in the background. A line of benches through Central Park. One of the bridges that lead in and out of the city. A picture of two people kissing. I pull the photo closer and study the profiles. It's David, but it must be from years ago. He sort of looks like a late-'90s Backstreet Boy—baggy jeans, boxy leather jacket. His arm outstretched toward the bottom left-hand side of the image, holding the camera. The girl has long red hair in a messy side braid escaping her coat's white furry hood. I look closer, trying to imagine David in love. Then my breath catches in my throat. The beauty mark. Under her right earlobe. It's Mom. My hands shake. But Mom kissing David? It can't be.

I turn the photo over but there's nothing on the back. No clue as to when this was taken. But it's definitely Mom. The hair, the skin, the eyes, even shut, I know they're hers. I know it's her. She has to be in her twenties. But why is she kissing him? I should put the photo back, pretend I never saw it. Surely it's no big deal. I think back to Ben surprise-kissing me on the lips that day at the hospital in the parking lot, months ago. How Dylan totally got the wrong idea. But how it meant nothing to me— how I was so *over* Ben and totally into Dylan. But what if someone had captured that? What if I had a daughter and she found a photo of that years later? She would've assumed the worst, that I was with *Ben* instead of Dylan. Just like I'm doing, right now.

Maybe Mom knew David first. Before Dad. Maybe they dated before Dad?

But of course they didn't. They all met the same night. She and Dad started dating immediately. That's the story she told me, the same story Dad told me, the same story David told me. So a joke? But who joke-kisses someone they don't even like? I stick the photo in my back pocket and continue sweeping the rest into the box.

"Sure you're OK in there?" David calls.

"Yeah, I just . . . dropped something."

"Need help?"

"No!" I say a little too quickly, a little too loudly.

Mom's working the day shift, so I have to wait, under my Sabres blanket, in agony (or technically, in Greeneland, which actually feels like a million miles away from Mom) until she gets home at six to talk to her, even though I've left her three messages and a billion texts telling her to call me on a break. Good thing I'm not being held for ransom.

"I saw . . ." Now that I've got her on the phone, I can't say the words.

"You saw what?" Mom says, but she's distracted. Which is maybe better than having her full attention. I feel less panicky all of a sudden. I take a deep breath.

"A picture of you and David."

"Oh?" she says, breezily. As though it's nothing. So it must be nothing. I almost let it drop.

Because I don't want to know.

Except, I do.

"Kissing," I say before I lose my nerve.

Silence.

"Oh Pippa . . ." Mom says.

"Did you two . . . have a *thing*?"

"I . . . oh Pippa . . . I was a model. I kissed a lot of guys. Wait. That came out wrong. Don't get any ideas. Or do. It's just kissing."

"But Dad's best friend? Really?"

"Please try not to think about it. It was nothing," she says. "It's nothing that matters now. I need to eat something. Can we talk about this later?"

"I think my mom and David had an affair," I blurt out as soon as Dace answers her phone. Ramona got home from class and tried to get me to come with her to dinner, but I refused and she said she'd bring me back mac 'n' cheese. The dorm room is empty again.

"Oh my god, *what*?"

"Hang on." I snap a pic of the photo, then text it to her. A second later I hear the ding on her end of the line. "Check my text." I hold my breath as she does, hoping she'll come back on the line telling me it's nothing, telling me not to worry or having some idea what the photo really means, something I didn't think of, something that's totally plausible.

"Wow. Who knew? What do you think it means?" She says, pulling a Dr. Judy.

"Well, I don't know. Except David even told me himself he didn't know Mom before she met Dad. So . . ."

"OK so maybe . . . they left out part of the story. Maybe she dated David for a bit? But it was, like, not a big deal?"

"Then why not say that?"

"'Cause it's weird. Parents always lie about their misspent youth. And David's not going to be all like, 'Hey, I know your dad's dead, but I banged your mom before they hooked up.'"

I groan.

"Feel better?"

I can't sleep. I want to call Dylan, to hear his voice, to hear him tell me it means nothing, but I know I can't—or that I shouldn't—call him, not even for this, and so I put my phone under my pillow and then flop over onto my back and stare at the ceiling. I know I should just accept that the kiss means nothing, but I can't. I would feel totally betrayed if Dace kissed Dylan, even if it was just as a joke. The photo's on my desk, and I alternate between looking at it, trying to look for clues as to what was going on outside that split second that's captured in the image, and flipping it over so that I don't have to see it. It's right beside the framed pic of Dad, and I feel guilty, even though I didn't do anything. I flip off my light, turn over and squeeze my eyes shut.

CHAPTER 14

Ramona convinces me to come back to class in the morning. Gabrielle doesn't say anything when she sees me—Ramona told her I wasn't feeling well, but I think we both know I skipped yesterday afternoon because of my evaluation. We spend the morning in the darkroom, which is a good thing because then I can't stare at the clock, waiting till we're let out for lunch so I can go to David's. He said I had to be there by 12:30 if I wanted to help with the sneaker-ad shoot, and when Gabrielle finally opens the revolving door to the darkroom and I squint in the bright light of the hallway, I see it's nearly quarter after. I practically run to David's, getting there in record time, but when I try his apartment door it's locked. I hit David's name on my phone. No answer. Same thing happens the third, fourth and fifth times. Where is he? Out picking up something last minute for the shoot?

Behind me, the crashing of wood and grate means the elevator's arrived at this floor. From the elevator's mouth appears a girl. Older than me, but not much. Maybe 22. Motorcycle boots, black tights with a rip in the right shin, some sort of black cape thing, enormous glasses, a black bob. Lugging a black box, she mumbles, "Excuse me," basically pushes me out of the way and tries the door. "Shit," she says, then pulls out her phone.

"I just tried him," I tell her.

She says "Westerly" like it's a swear word. Then: "Who are you?"

"He's my mentor. So I'm his, um, mentee? I guess. I'm at this photography camp at Tisch. He said I could assist—"

She looks me up and down. "Just stop. God, he's so disgusting. He gets older every year but they keep staying the same age."

"It's not like that—"

"Oh, don't defend him. Listen, I just want to do this shoot. He's done this before. And we probably should've booked a full day for this as it is. I'm Lauren, by the way."

The two of us lean against the wall by David's door for a while, and I consider how another photography fail will affect my chances of ever getting into Tisch after high school. I check my phone again, which is rather unnecessary since it's fully charged and still no calls and, yes, it's nearly 1:00 but I know that because Lauren's been saying things like "12:45, 12:46, 12:47 . . ." with exasperated sighs in between every minute on the minute.

Lauren's phone buzzes with a text. "Great. And now the talent will be here any minute."

"What happens then?"

Lauren doesn't appear to hear me over her moaning; she's getting apocalyptic on me. "My parents said I'd end up selling my body if I moved to New York. Is that really what's going to have to happen? I don't want to be a call girl, but is this how it happens? Is this what happens to innocent girls, coming to New York, trying to make it as actresses, dancers, singers? They trust the wrong person, one wrong turn, and that's that? Ugh, why did I have to beg the agency to book David?"

"Lauren, I've got an idea." I lead her up the stairs and there's a hatch to the roof, which turns out to be covered in tarpaper, with empty beer bottles and lawn chairs decorating the flat area beneath a rusty water tower. Lauren follows me to the roof edge, and the two of us look over at David's balcony below. Where a sliding door beckons.

"What if the door's locked?"

"He's a smoker—maybe there's a chance he left the door unlocked?"

"I'll hold you," Lauren says.

"Why don't you do it?"

"I'm afraid of heights."

Which is why seconds later I'm up on the edge and then on my belly and my legs are dangling with maybe eight feet between my own motorcycle boots and the balcony below. Which doesn't sound like much. Eight feet—that's not even the height of a basketball net, right? I don't think? Oh, how would

I know? Who do I think I am—Lebron James? Dace would probably know, but Dace isn't here, and I've got to focus. Anyway, it seems far, particularly when it's December and icy and I can hear New York below, with all its honking and sirens. Waiting for me to fall.

"You're not going to fall," Lauren says instinctively, pressing herself against the edge of the roof and I kind of use her as a rope ladder, lowering myself from her shoulder, to her elbow, to her wrist, I'm dangling in space and then I drop—and fall three feet to the balcony.

"Are you OK?" she calls.

"I think I'm OK."

"You sound surprised."

"I *am* surprised."

The balcony door's open. In fact, I beat Lauren to the front door. When I open it she's just coming out the stairs and down the hallway and her face breaks into a smile as she strides my way. "I cannot *believe* that worked."

Inside the studio, it's clear David's not just a really heavy and late sleeper. There's no sign of him, though the place is a disaster, like he had a party last night, then abandoned the place. Beer bottles, pizza boxes, cigarette packs litter the floor. I confess to being a little concerned about him but Lauren shrugs, seemingly disinterested. "Photo camp. So you can handle a camera?"

"Sure."

"Great. The models are going to be here in 15

minutes. Here's the project sheet. I'll get the clothes. Let's get to it."

It's while I read the project sheet that it becomes apparent to me why Lauren asked whether I can handle a camera—because in her mind, we are going ahead with this and she wants me to shoot whatever we're shooting. Like, we're not canceling even if David doesn't show up. Because, of course, who else is there? I study the sheet, hoping for some clue as to what, and *how* I'm supposed to do this.

Project Sheet

ZePPys are a new line of athletic-style shoes. But they're not just shoes. And they're definitely not boring. And they're most certainly not for adults. Designed to appeal to the pre-teen set, ZePPys will make you ZANY + PEPPY. Get it?! ZePPy! The campaign is based around bright, bold images. The tweens should be zany! They should be peppy! They should be ZePPy!

It's awful. It can't just be me, can it? This sounds like a terrible campaign. What pre-teen wants to feel zany or peppy? And I feel full-fledged stressed out. In fact, I feel about five seconds from needing a Dr. Judy intervention.

"I think . . . what if . . . what if we just postpone?" I text David again.

Lauren's bustling around the studio, doing this, doing that, I have no idea what, I'm so unfocused.

"You're doing it."

"But what if I don't do a good job?" I want to say *How can I do a good job when this is what I have to work with?*

"You have to do a good job." Lauren goes back to setting up the clothes on the rack.

"But won't this ruin David's reputation if I screw this up for him? It's totally unrealistic. I'm not a real photographer. I can't just *step in* and take over an actual shoot for someone like David. Not for an actual shoe campaign. Not for a real ad agency." Is Lauren crazy?

But she just tilts her head and looks at me, holding a hanger with a white tuxedo shirt. "Did you *read* the shoot sheet? It's not like I just handed you a Nike campaign."

Is that supposed to make me feel better? But it's clear Lauren's serious about me shooting this thing. This *campaign.*

I look at my phone again. Nothing from David. I pull up Ramona's name.

Me: Help.

Ramona: What's up?

Me: I need u. Can u come here?

Ramona: U OK??? Shooting look book with Jed!

Me: Can u come after? Really need help. Will owe u.

And seriously not 20 minutes later Ramona shows up. With Ben. I don't even have time to ask her *why* or *how* that came together, because all I can focus on is how they thankfully beat the models and hair/makeup team to the loft. They take the situation in stride, both of them, and I'm so glad they're both here—yes, that's right, I'm so glad Ben's here—that I hug them both. Does Ben hold me for a second longer than a couple of friends might hug? I don't have the time to ponder it. Ben goes around rustling up more lights from the storage closet, while Ramona tidies up the beer and pizza mess. Lauren sets the sneakers up. They're highlighted in electric shades—neon orange, that sort of thing—and so I get the orange seamless and roll that out, and by that time Kat and Maxi—not the models' real names, their fun and zany names for the campaign—are getting their hair and makeup done. An hour later they're ready: Kat's kind of a spy-looking figure in a tux. She carries a gun. A fake gun, obviously. At least I hope it's a fake gun. Maxi's in a slinky cocktail dress, all sequins, which looks ridiculous on her, given that she's 13, tops. The models' agency rep doesn't seem to notice—or care?—that Ramona, Ben and I are in charge of this shoot, or that we're teenagers. Maybe he thinks it's all part of the zeppyness? Anyway, he's on the couch, engrossed in his phone.

The models' rep might not care how the shoot turns out, but the agency will if the client thinks the work is amateurish, unprofessional. Lauren's stressed. How am I going to guarantee that the agency—a well-established agency that has used

David for multiple campaigns—will like my stuff? That they won't see through it and know I'm a complete newbie, that I've duped them. And before I know it, I'm sitting down, on the floor, back against the concrete wall. Head between my knees.

"Pippa!" Ramona hisses. "What are you doing?"

What *am* I doing? That's the question of the hour. "How can I do this?"

"Remember Olivia Bee?" Ramona says, sitting down in front of me.

"Who?" I say, and then I remember. Olivia Bee, the girl who when she was, like, 15, got discovered through her photos on Flickr and got a contract to shoot a Converse sneaker ad.

Only, there's a huge difference between Converse and . . . ZePPys.

Or is there? Is it what I make of the ad? I've got to make it my own.

"Guys, I think we better start shooting," Ben says, and I look up and he's nodding over at the models' rep, who's looking around.

That's all it takes, and I'm up on my feet, ready to own this campaign. I can do this. I've been at enough shoots with Dace to know what works and what doesn't, and these girls, they're *kids*. They're laughing and snapping selfies on their phones. And, as far as I can tell, don't seem to have any sort of diva-esque attitude. So all I've got to do is get them to be zany. And peppy.

"All right, girls," I say, and the girls actually look over at me. They stand up, and I walk over to them. I explain the campaign, how it's supposed to go. How

Kat's supposed to be a spy, how Maxi's supposed to be a socialite. How they're very serious about their very serious lifestyles. But then, the shoes. They're wearing these shoes, and they're quirky, they're fun. They're unexpected. The girls nod, totally getting it, and I move them into place. I squeeze off a few frames as Ramona works the lights and the bounce card and Ben works the fan and Lauren fixes wardrobe, and Amy and Jae, the hair and makeup girls, get in there, fixing flyaways and adding more blush, and maybe half an hour later, I pause and we gather round the computer to review the first of the lot. And it's funny. But the young models in their sort of ridiculous outfits? Dare I say it? They look . . . a little zany. A little peppy.

Eventually, Lauren says she thinks we've got enough coverage and the rep's out of there in a flash, not even asking to see the photos. The hair and makeup girls start packing up their kits, and Ramona leads the girls to get changed. Ben's moving the lights out of the way. The girls come out of the bathroom, back in their street clothes, and Ramona starts putting their clothes back on the rack. Ben asks them if they want a snack from the kitchen. I turn my attention to Lauren.

"Wow, this might've been the most productive shoot I've ever done in David's place."

"Really?" I say hopefully.

"Yeah for sure. OK so now you've got to pick three photos. So here's a tip: don't pick the best ones, necessarily," she says as we scroll through them. "Maybe one that's really strong, the other two can just be pretty good. Don't labor over it. Just send three pretty good ones to the client"—she opens the mail icon on the computer and thankfully, it doesn't need a password—"OK, great. We can send it from David's email—they'll never know the difference. You want to impress them enough that they're pleased, but leave a few better shots to send through later."

She checks her phone. "I've got to go. Are you going to be OK to do this on your own?"

"Wait, you're leaving?" But she's already throwing a few random items—notebook, pen, her phone—into her Marc Jacobs bag and slinging it over her shoulder.

"You can do it."

And then it's there: that old familiar feeling, that sense of panic rising up, but a second later, without much effort, I'm squelching it, pushing it down and nodding confidently. "No problem. Thanks for all your help on this," I say, as though I really am in charge here.

"You were great. OK, I'm out of here."

She heads out, Amy and Jae following her, and then it's just Ramona, Ben and me. I wave them over to the computer. We huddle around and start to go through the pics. There's a nervous energy in the air—none of us are talking about anything else, none of us are really talking at all. We're just studying the pics in front of us, one by one.

"I think you should pick three different styles," Ramona says. "That way you have a better chance the client likes one of them."

"That's a good idea," I say, and so we all lean a

little closer. Ramona points at one, Ben points at another, and we start flagging them, narrowing down the pics, and then going back over them again, the ones flagged red getting an extra yellow flag if they're going to make it to the final six. And then we choose three, I attach them to an email and hit send.

Then we wait, breathless for the client to reply. Eventually, the computer dings with a new message. I click on the mail icon.

Looks great. Can't wait to see the rest.

Ramona hugs me first and then I turn, and Ben's standing behind me and I hug him.

"We did it," I say, and Ben shakes his head.

"You did it."

"It's true," Ramona says. "You really did it. You were, like, a real photographer."

I smile, and then I laugh.

"What's so funny?" Ramona says, looking at me like I'm crazy. I shake my head.

"I don't know. I just feel . . . so much relief."

"You're a freak," Ben says, but not unkindly. More, like, in awe. And then he laughs. And then Ramona laughs, and then we're all laughing. God, it feels good to laugh.

Ben puts his phone on the iPod dock and a second later Daft Punk pumps through the speakers. We start cleaning up.

Ramona's in the kitchen, tidying up the dishes, and Ben's lugging a seamless back to the storage room, and every so often one of us moves to the music. And we're sort of half-dancing, half-cleaning up. Totally having fun.

"I still can't believe we pulled it off," I say, rolling up the final seamless.

"Here, let me get that," Ben says, taking the other end, and we carry it into the storage room. As we lean it up against the wall, the seamless knocks over the shoebox for the second time this week. Ramona bends down, flips the box right-side up, and I crouch down, then sit back against the shelves on the left. I ask Ramona to leave the box for a minute. Ben senses something's up, and he sits too, the three of us facing each other, a little impromptu pow-wow. And so I spill it—the details of what the shoebox contained.

"Whoa," Ramona says.

Ben's silent for a moment. "So . . . your mom had an affair with your mentor?"

"She claims she didn't—that it was just a kiss. Chaste."

"Yeah right," Ramona says. "Do you have the pic?"

The photo is in my bag. I go out into the studio, pull it out, bring it back into the storage closet. The three of us stare at it awhile.

"She looks pretty happy," Ben says.

"Yeah," I say. "But is she happy like, 'Wow, it's so much fun to hang out with David Westerly, my good friend, my boyfriend's friend. So great that he's not a big jerk, which would be a super drag,' OR, is she happy, like, 'Wow, I'm so in love with David Westerly even though he's my boyfriend's best friend and this is wrong, so wrong'?"

Silence as we contemplate this. I study the

photo—Mom's body language, her eyes—searching for a clue.

"It could go either way," Ramona says just as Ben's like, "We need more evidence."

After a pause, I point to the shoebox. "We *have* more evidence. That's David Westerly's time capsule of love. There's probably something else in there."

"So what are we waiting for?" Ben asks. He looks at Ramona. "Right?" She looks at me. I nod, and each of us grasps a stack of . . . stuff, I guess you'd call it? Notes and restaurant receipts and sports game tickets and theater playbills. Birthday cards and postcards and business cards and a single, distressed credit card that expired more than five years ago.

"It's funny," Ben says, looking at the photo that started of all this. "If I didn't know, I'd say the person you're related to in this photo isn't your mom, it's David. You kind of—I don't know—there's some resemblance. Like him just being around rubbed off on you, even before you were born? Anyway, photos are totally deceiving. Case in point."

"What's your mom's name again?" Ramona asks, and I tell her.

"Holly Masterson," she repeats. "That's a great name."

"He went to a lot of concerts," Ben observes. "Pearl Jam, Nirvana, the Pixies, Radiohead, Oasis, Beastie Boys. Run-DMC at Madison Square Gardens—these are a lot of big shows at the time."

Did Mom go with him to these shows? It's funny to think about my mom at a concert—without Dad.

"You know what we need? A love letter. That would be the smoking gun," Ben says.

"Holly Masterson," Ramona's saying, again.

She has a paper in her hand. She shows me the back—and there's my mom's name. In black letters.

"That's her," I say. "What is it?"

"Flip it over," Ramona says.

I do, and I'm looking at a ghostly black and white outline of a creature, something like an alien, small body, large head.

"It's an ultrasound," Ramona says.

A string of numbers lines the bottom. A date, I realize when I see the year. I do the math. Six months before I was born.

I stare at it. Finally, I put the photo down on the concrete ground.

"Guys," I say slowly, "I think this is me."

Ben and Ramona don't want to leave me alone, but I tell them, "I'm fine!" though is anyone ever *fine* when they say they're fine?—but anyway, I tell them I want to go to Emmy's to talk to her, and so they head back to the dorm, and since I don't want to risk getting caught at David's, holding the ultrasound photo, if and when he ever shows up, I sit in the stairwell at the other end of the hall, the one that leads to the lofts on the other side of the building, and stare at the photo.

And then I do the one thing I was never supposed to do.

I text Dylan. But seriously?

REASONS TO BREAK AN ILL-THOUGHT-OUT COMMUNICATION BAN:

1. Finding out your father may not actually be your father.

Then, I stare at my phone. But the screen doesn't change. It's like it's frozen. No response. Nothing. *Nothing?* I get we had THE RULE and that he's busy being WITH THE BAND, but seriously? It's not like I texted *Hey, whatcha doing?* Or even *I miss you.*

What I texted was *I think David is my real father.* Which, to be fair, is pretty much as cryptic as cryptic texts go, since Dylan doesn't even know who David is. Like, *maybe* he'd remember, if I'd texted *David Westerly*, that he was the photographer-friend of my dad's (though not likely), but I didn't, I just texted "David" and he doesn't even *know* that David's a mentor in the program. Why? Because of the ILL-THOUGHT-OUT COMMUNICATION BAN. See how much happens in less than two weeks?

Still. You get a text that seems like it may be rewriting family history from your girlfriend *who you love*, and you don't respond just to check that it wasn't some sort of random autocorrect and that she's OK before going back to the ban?

I feel angry, then sad, then hurt. I'm basically working my way through a 12-step recovery program in about 12 seconds.

I hit the FaceTime app and call Dace.

When she answers I hold the photo up to the phone.

She leans in, squinting. "What is that?"

"A baby. Kind of. An ultrasound. I think . . . it's me."

Dace leans even closer to her screen. "*What*?"

I give her the details.

"Wow. Wow. So this, plus the kiss . . ."

"I don't know what to think. I'm being crazy, right? Like the kiss was no big deal, and somehow David got a copy of my ultrasound from my mom and dad. Like, maybe my dad came right here after they got the ultrasound—he had a shoot, or he wanted to show David 'cause he was super excited—and he left it here, and he thought he lost it and David never knew he had it and years passed and David found it and always meant to pop it in the mail. But he never got around to it. It's not like he's moved five times and purposely packed it up and took it to the new place. He probably has unpaid parking tickets from 16 years ago, old socks with holes, right?"

Dace looks totally perplexed.

"Right, Dace? I need you to say, 'Yes, it's totally plausible, that makes sense, you're overreacting, it's nothing more than that.'"

After a long pause, Dace says finally, "Yeah well, you're not gonna get that from me. Honesty Pact, being your best friend, and all . . ." She stands up.

"Where are you going?"

She grabs a pad of yellow legal paper off her desk. "Let's make a list."

"Of what?"

"The facts. Fact: David has an ultrasound of you."

"OK."

"Fact: David is a lefty."

At least I know Dace has been listening during my gushfests about David. Dace puts her pen in her mouth and types something into her computer, then looks back at me. "Did you know only 1 in 10 people in the world are lefties? And that you can't be a lefty unless there's someone in your family who's also a lefty. Who in your family is also a lefty?"

My chest hurts. "Are you making this up?"

Dace shakes her head, leaning into her computer. "No. Fact: David is from Philadelphia."

"Yes, but *lots* of people are from Philadelphia." I open my browser and Google the population of Philadelphia. "To be exact, 1.5 million people."

"But not your mom or dad."

"It's true." I bite my lip. "And well, they've never even been there."

"What?" Dace asks. "They've never *been* to the place they named you after? How did I *not* know this? I just assumed they were pulling a Posh and Becks, you know, for where you were conceived. Like Brooklyn Beckham. Only not so glam."

"They always said they just liked the way it rolled off the tongue."

"Um, *Phil-a-del-phi-a* doesn't roll off the tongue."

"OK, but we're forgetting the other facts. Write this down: Mom hates David."

Dace shakes her head. "Not valid. You hated Ben two weeks ago. As far as Dylan knows, you still do. And look how much things have changed in a week and a half."

"I'm just being nice to him. I'm being a nice person."

"Mm hmm. I'm just saying . . . what if you were your mom, and Dylan were your dad? Ben would be David."

"I'm not having sex with Ben. I'm not even having sex with Dylan."

"Yeah, but you're 16, not 21. And remember my theory: hate isn't the opposite of love. Indifference is. Hate means there's still passion."

"OK, what's your point? What are you saying? That my mom and dad have been lying to me my entire life?"

"I'm just saying . . . what if?"

"Oh god." This what-if is too big to ignore.

CHAPTER 15

The next morning I'm not doing any better with the
big what-if factor. I consider staying in my room
but Ramona talks me out of it, which is probably
for the best, I guess, so that I don't let my mind go
straight to the whirlpool of what-ifs, but going to
class doesn't do anything to take my mind off David,
Mom, Dad and that ultrasound.

Still, I somehow manage to keep it together in
class, through lunch, through our field trip to the
Guggenheim. I even keep it together when Ben and
Ramona and I are taking the subway back and Ben
looks over at me midway through the strobing,
shuddering ride and sees me gripping the metal pole
in the center of the train and biting my lip and he
edges a little closer and just as we're entering a dark
portion of the ride he wraps his free arm around me
and holds me, tight, close, not saying anything, and I

close my eyes and I think about my dad and my mom and the nice guy and the bad guy and the way love is crazy, which is a saying I've heard many times before and not understood. Love is crazy. Sometimes you fall in love with someone and it doesn't make sense. Is that what happened to Holly Masterson?

I'm sitting on Emmy's front steps, still keeping it together, when she gets home from work. "What a great surprise!" she says. And then I break. It's massive, ugly-cry time. One hiccup of a lung-splitting sob. Another. Emmy drops her bag on the sidewalk and rushes to me.

"What happened? Who? What? Oh god." Emmy is legitimately freaking out. And I realize that I'm alone, in New York, sobbing on her steps. That can't look good.

"I'm OK," I splutter, so she doesn't think I've been mugged. Or worse. "I just need to talk."

She sits beside me on the steps, pulling me into her, squeezing me tight. "It's freezing out here. Let's get you inside." She pulls me up, and I follow her into her building. Once upstairs, she closes the door, pulls my coat off me. "Tea?"

I nod, kick off my boots and put my hat and mitts on the chair by the door, then walk over to the couch. She puts on the kettle, then comes over and sits beside me. I swipe at my eyes and blow my nose on a tissue she hands me. Then I hold out the ultrasound photo. She takes it. Studies it, turns it over, looks at me.

"Is it possible to love two people at the same time?" I ask.

"Oh god," she says. "Yes. Sure. But what does that have to do with this?"

"Everything. Nothing. I don't know. Is that me?"

She studies my face. The kettle whistles and she gets up, turns the burner off and pours the hot water into a pot for tea.

"I know it's me. Mom's name, the date—of course it's me. My real question is why does David have it? Why does David have my ultrasound?"

Emmy returns with a tray and sits back down beside me on the couch.

"You should talk to your mom."

"I can't. I need you to tell me the truth."

She pours tea in two cups, hands one to me. "I . . . Pippa, it's not my place to tell you. It's none of my business."

"You have to. I . . . I just want to know. I don't want Mom to know that I know. She's obviously kept this from me for a reason. But I have a right to know, don't I? If David's my father?"

"Pippa . . ." Emmy blows on her tea. How can she drink tea? I want to, want to believe it will take the world's problems away, but it feels implausible. I set my cup on the table.

"She cheated on Dad?" My voice quivers. "So what, she wasn't sure about Dad? She was going to break up with him? Did he even know that I wasn't his real daughter?" Another tear escapes. "Or he knew and he just . . . he just let her get away with it?

He stayed with her even though she had *sex* with his best friend?" Suddenly it all makes sense. Why Mom doesn't like David. Why Dad and David never saw each other anymore. "Or does she even know who the father is? I don't know whether to hate Mom or Dad more. I feel so betrayed and, like, I don't even know them."

"Pippa, that's not how it happened. Not even close." She puts her cup back on the table, then places a hand on my knee.

"How else could it have happened? Mom met Dad, dated him, cheated on him with David and had me. The only thing I don't know is whether Dad knew what Mom did to him." I shake my head. "How can I go home and face Mom? I don't—I don't even want to go home." The tears are coming quicker now. I swipe at my cheek with the back of my hand.

Emmy swivels me to face her, gripping my shoulders with her hands. "You don't understand, Pippa. Your mother never cheated on Evan. She . . ." She trails off, then pulls me close and hugs me. Outside there's the incessant honking of an irate driver, but inside, it's quiet, the only sound the hum of the refrigerator. I wait, hoping that Emmy just tells the truth. Finally, she pulls away from me, looks at me, her mouth a straight line across her face.

"OK, listen," she says seriously, then inhales deeply. Exhales. "I'm going to tell you what I know. The truth I know."

My breath catches. I'm frozen, afraid to move, afraid to lose this moment, whatever is persuading Emmy to tell me what she knows. I watch her, as she releases her grip on me, then fiddles with the hem of her shirt. Takes another deep breath. And then she starts.

"Your mother met David and your father at the same time. David and your dad were best friends, yes. But it was your mother and David who started dating each other first."

I let this sink in. Emmy watches me.

"My mom was with David before she was with my dad?" I clarify.

"That's right."

"But that's crazy."

"Why?"

"She never talked about it with me."

"Would she, though? Has she ever talked about any of the boyfriends she had before she met your dad?"

"I just assumed she never had any boyfriends before Dad."

"Pippa . . ." Emmy smiles, and now that I've said it, it does sound naïve. "You know how beautiful your mother is. And when she was young, she was even more beautiful. She was . . . vivacious."

I think about Mom, back before Dad got sick, when she wore skinny jeans and makeup and they'd go on dates. And then, she just sort of let herself go. "She isn't exactly vivacious anymore."

"Cut your mom some slack right now. And I'm not talking even the last few years . . . Well, people change." She looks down at her tea. Emmy sighs. "Should I put out some cookies?"

Answers? Yes. Cookies? Not so much.

I shake my head but Emmy gets up anyway. "Just going to get more milk," she says. But instead, she just stands there at the counter in the kitchen. Long moments pass. Eventually she returns, setting the creamer on the table and sighing as she sits down again.

"People fall in love, they break up, they fall in love again. Are you going to be with Ben for the rest of your life?"

"Ben?" Have I mentioned Ben so much to Emmy that she thinks *he's* my boyfriend? "I'm not with Ben. My boyfriend's Dylan."

"Right, sorry. OK—are you going to be with Dylan for the rest of your life?"

"I thought so, yeah. I thought we were going to be like my mom and dad. True love. Together forever."

Emmy stands. "Do you want to walk? I could use some fresh air."

I don't respond, but I get up and follow Emmy to the door. We slip our shoes back on, grab our coats, and then we're out, down the stairs and onto the street. It's already dark. Emmy turns right and I walk beside her.

"Pip, your mother was the kind of girl boys fell in love with the moment they saw her. She had plenty of boyfriends."

"But she was only ever in love with my dad?"

"Oh Pippa, wouldn't that be so simple if that were the case? But no. Your mother was in love with David first. And before David there were other loves. She was a model in New York in the '90s.

She had plenty of love affairs. Did she ever tell you about the time she dated Moby?"

"Who's Moby?"

"The musician?" We cross a busy intersection. "He had a tea shop. He was very cool. You know he's a photographer too—published a book of photographs from his tour a few years ago, did a show in Hollywood."

"OK, great, fine. Why didn't it work out with that dude?" I say, getting more confused by the minute.

"He was going through a cleanse. Which entailed not showering. He smelled terrible. OK, we are totally off topic. Her other boyfriends are not the point."

There's a silence while about a billion different thoughts buzz through my head.

"David and Holly started dating after they met that night at the bar. They fell in love. Your mother loved him, she truly did. But David . . ."

"What?"

"He was David. He was exactly like how David is now. He loved your mother, for sure, but he was a player. He was good looking and knew it. All the girls loved him. He was the male version of your mother, in some ways. Just as full of life as she was."

"My mom? A player?"

"Well, didn't want to be tied down is maybe a better description. And why should she be? She was so young." I dodge a guy on a bike coming toward me. People behind me shout at him to get off the sidewalk.

"They must've made quite the pair," I say, thinking about how pretty Mom was when she was young. And how cute David was. Like Mila and Ashton, maybe? Or Leo and his supermodel of the moment?

"They would walk into a party and, you think I'm kidding but seriously, the conversation would stop. I've never seen anything like it. They turned heads like no one else."

"What about my dad? Was he in love with someone else too?"

"Well, that was a funny thing. Your father was always around. He was never dating anyone else, not as long as I knew him. I always thought it was kind of weird, because he didn't actually seem like he *liked* being alone. It felt like he wanted to be with someone but just . . . couldn't find the right girl."

Snow is starting to fall. I do up the top button of my coat. We keep walking for a while, a few blocks, neither of us saying anything. A storefront plays "Silver Bells" as we pass.

"So how did they end up together—Mom and Dad?" I say finally. "Mom . . . cheated?" I hate the idea that Mom's still a cheater, but at least with this story, Dad's actually my dad, and David's just some weird ultrasound collector.

"Pippa, no. Not at all. These are things you should ask your mother."

"Emmy, my mother's kept this secret from me for 16 years. You think she's suddenly going to tell me the truth when I ask?"

"David's been your mentor, this week, right?"

"Yeah."

"Is he reliable? Dependable?"

"Well . . . what do you mean?"

"Has he shown up to everything on time? Totally acting professional?"

I think back to yesterday, to the photo shoot we had to save for him. Because of him. And all I got in return was a *Thx* and a vague *See u later* text in response. I had fun and whether Mikael and Gabrielle like the work I did or not, I know *I* actually learned something. But yeah, he should've been there. Even the first day to meet me, he was late.

"I guess he's been pretty flaky." I relay the past week and a bit.

"Sounds about right. Your mom thought she could change him. Oh, she was so in love with him. Or infatuated with him. One or the other. And then she found out she was pregnant, and she told David, and they made plans to move in together. They did—she moved into his place, the studio." I'm surprised. All this time, the studio, I'd been picturing Dad there, but it was Mom who was actually living in it. I try to picture her there, pregnant with me.

"This was about three months before you were born. She moved into his studio, and for a while we all thought it might work out. That somehow she'd changed him. Or he'd changed himself. He seemed like a reformed man. He stopped staying out until 4 a.m. He turned down this great gig in London to stay with Holly. He went with her to buy a stroller."

The London internship. The girl was Mom.

"They were happy?"

"Happy? Oh god, I don't know about happy.

They were two intense people at an intense time of their lives, and they'd have these intense fights and intense reconciliations. One time your mom called me up in Spalding, just because she needed someone to talk to, and I asked her why she stayed with him. Or—no, what I said was 'You must really love him to stay with him through all that fighting.' And I'll never forget what your mom said."

Silence fills the space between us, for what seems like forever. We're just walking. It feels like we've been walking on this street forever. We're on Avenue of the Americas, passing big building after big building. There aren't many shops, not like on 5th.

Finally I feel the need to fill it. "You're going to tell me, right?"

"I'm just trying to get it right. She said, 'Love?' But in this way, like it was a foreign concept to her. She said, 'Love? When there's a baby involved, maybe you have to give up on love.' And then you were born."

I wince a little thinking about how hard it must've been for my mom; no wonder she never mentioned the loveless part of my origin story. "Mom said it was a hard birth."

"It was, and your mom stayed in the hospital for a few days—she had to be monitored—and David, very dutifully, stayed with her until the last night. He was supposed to go home and get everything ready. The nurses discharged your mom the following morning, and David was supposed to pick her up and he didn't show. She had to take a taxi to the studio, by herself. When she got home—"

"There was a woman there." I know it. I can't even imagine Mom walking in with a baby and some other girl, a Talia, standing there. But Emmy shakes her head.

"There was no one there. An empty studio, an unmade bed, the stroller still in the box—not exactly the homecoming you want your baby to have."

"Where was he?"

Emmy shrugs.

"So she broke up with him?"

"Basically. He showed up a day or two later, but by that time she'd packed up everything into a couple of bags. She couldn't rely on him, so she decided to go where she could have someone to rely on. Someone to count on. Back home. To our mom and dad. Your grandma and grandpa." Emmy stops and rubs my back, just like my mom does when I'm upset. "Your dad and I helped her get you and the rest of her stuff into a cab, and your dad went with her to the bus station. That was supposed to be it. Your mom would get on the bus to Spalding, move back into our house, that was it. She'd never see David or your dad again."

"Oh god."

We turn into a plaza, and I realize we're at the Rockefeller Center. The Christmas tree shoots into the night sky in front of us. There has to be at least a thousand lights on the tree. We approach the railing, the one with flags of the world all around it, and stand overlooking the ice rink below. It's packed with couples holding hands, single people, skating all in the same direction. A girl in a white fur-trimmed coat does a spin in the middle. Like we're on the set of a movie. I stare, waiting for Emmy to go on.

"Holly was crying while she was holding you, just about to get on the bus, and your dad took both of you in his arms on the platform. One last hug. And who knows what it was—maybe it was the smell of her hair? Maybe it was you swaddled in your little receiving blankets. Maybe it was the fumes from all that bus exhaust? But your dad found the courage to tell your mom what he'd hidden from her as long as he'd known her. He told her he loved her, that he would always love her. That he would spend the rest of his life trying and failing to find a girl who lived up to Holly Masterson. Your mom was blown away—she'd just been abandoned by the guy she thought she'd be with forever—the father of her child. She'd thought that would be the start of their family together, a real family. And here she was, alone. And then, suddenly, here was this friend of hers professing his love, not only for her, but also for her baby, because he did that too. He told her he would love you forever."

My breath catches. "And what happened?"

"He got on the bus with her. He helped her settle in Spalding, and you know the rest—he stayed. He was true to his word. Your dad was always true to his word. And your mom loved him back. The bus trip was so easy with your dad, when something like that would have been hell with David. I think there was a part of her that always knew.

"And that was that. They had no money, and your father still had his place in New York, this place, and

I'd been planning to move to New York after I finished high school anyway, so we kind of switched,
and I moved in here, and Grandma and Grandpa let
your father move in with them, and your dad figured
out how to make a business with his photography
in Spalding. And all of a sudden they were this little
family. And it was like it was always meant to be.
They knew each other so well, they'd been friends
for so long—it was like they were just meant to be
together. And then they were."

Neither of us says anything for a few moments.
As it all sinks in. I lean over the railing, hands on it,
breathing in the cold night air.

"So that's why Mom was always weird about
David," I say finally, turning to Emmy. She nods.

"She's always been worried that he would try to
come back into your lives, that he'd try to be your
father. Not because she didn't want you to know
who your real father was, but because . . ." she trails
off. "Well, she was sure that if David tried to be
your father, that he would mess it up somehow and
let you down. And your father was a natural. Your
mother didn't want your dad—who was *being* your
dad every single day, just like you were his own—to
be hurt by David's actions."

"What about Dad? Did he ever talk to David
again?" As much as Dad always praised David's
work, I realize I have no idea if they ever spoke,
ever saw each other. I always assumed they did,
in that way that you don't really think about who
your parents email or talk to when you're not paying
attention, but now I wonder if that was when their

friendship ended. If all Dad ever had left was nostalgia. Even that seems hard to swallow, though.

"Of course their friendship was never the same—for so many reasons. But David wasn't upset with your father for being with your mom, and your father, he wasn't one to hold grudges. To say things happen for a reason feels like such a cliché. It *is* such a cliché but in this case, I've always thought, maybe it really rings true. How could your dad really hate David for what he did, if it meant he ended up with the woman he always loved and a child he loved so, so dearly? And he wanted you to know David's work too—to be inspired by David and look up to him, even if he wasn't going to be a father to you."

"I always felt like I was the reason Dad wasn't as famous as David. And I guess I was right, I just didn't know the whole story."

Emmy hugs me as snow falls on us. "Your dad wouldn't have changed anything for the world."

CHAPTER 16

The next morning Ramona pulls me out of bed, basically dresses me, feeds me a mocha and a chocolate chip cookie and gets me to class. I can't imagine how I'll be able to focus on anything, especially when I keep checking my phone and *still* have no texts from Dylan. But when Mikael starts talking about the end of camp reception on Friday I realize that this camp— this *experience*—is almost over, and then I'm fully engaged. We have to exhibit something—but what, they're really leaving it up to us to decide. A single photo or a series, something we've already completed or something totally new, even if the instructors haven't seen it. After all the criticism of the week, this free for all seems kind of like the opposite of everything we've learned. "Show us what you've got. Give us the photos that represent you best. Not because we told you so, because you believe it. Photography is subjective. It's an art. But it's also a business. Show us you have what it takes to make it."

And so, we spend most of the day studying various techniques, and then we're on the computers learning photo-manipulation techniques, and then the day's over, and I realize tomorrow's our last night left. Before we go home.

I have an idea.

"I'll meet you at the dining hall," I tell Ramona when we're almost at the dorm. Then I take off in the other direction.

Times Square is totally different in the middle of the day. At night, the lights are the showstopper. They illuminate the sky so that it looks like day. But it's not reality. In daytime, the lights are still there, the ads still playing, the marquees with their scrolling messages still moving along, but it's not just about the lights. I look around, take in the people. Sure there are tourists—standing at the ticket booth, staring up at the signs—but that's not all.

I hold my camera up to my face and focus in on two guys, walking in suits, cutting through the Square, then entering the tall glass building on the corner of 46th and Broadway.

A group of girls in school uniforms stand in line to get into the Starbucks. Why didn't I notice before—it's not just a tourist trap. New York happens here, more than you expect. Is that what Dad liked about this place? Or was it something else?

I think about Dad, how he wasn't my dad, not technically. How he loved Mom, how he wanted to be with her, all that time. How his best friend was with the girl he wanted to be with, and when finally he wasn't, it wasn't an ideal situation—she's pregnant, leaving New York because she has to—and he didn't care. He wanted to be with her and that's all that mattered. Wanted to be her partner. Wanted to be a father to me.

I think back to not even two weeks ago. How different I thought this camp would turn out. How I thought I'd be *in* my element, not totally out of it. How different all of us are in the program, how we all had very different experiences being here. How I thought I wasn't even going to speak to Ben at all, and now, how I spent maybe the most time with him out of anyone else.

How life doesn't always unfold the way you think, the way you see it. There are layers. I hold my camera up and start snapping. Focusing not on the obvious, but on the unexpected, on the layers. Changing my depth of field.

CHAPTER 17

On Friday, our mini end-of-Tisch-Camp gala is set to start at 7, but we're all early, setting up, hanging out. Our mentors are supposed to come, but David isn't here yet. It doesn't matter. Not really. Ramona and I have put our photos up beside each other's. She's showing a series on movement. I have just one photo, enlarged and mounted on canvas. The caption on the little square of white paper beside it: *Times Square*. But it's not the typical view of the busiest spot in New York. The focus is a gold ring. A perfect circle of gold set against the asphalt. I got down on my stomach, shot it at eye level, the chairs, the garbage, the feet of dozens of tourists, locals and those who trek through Times Square every day blurred out in the background. Something lost? Something about to be found? Does it belong to someone who comes through every day, who will find it later today, or maybe tomorrow? Or does it belong to someone who came only once, on vacation, lost it and will never see it again? Or someone who purposely threw it away?

Mikael walks up behind me. We stand, side by side, taking in my photograph. Mikael's hands are clasped behind his back. His body still, impossible to read. Finally he says, "You've come a long way in two weeks, Ms. Greene." Then he turns and walks on to the next photograph.

I hide a smile as Connor walks past. "Looks like you earned your sweatshirt."

This time I'm not embarrassed. Because I *did*.

David never shows up, but it's not like I won't see him. He's hosting the afterparty, for all of us, mentors and students and instructors included, at his studio. Everyone's excited—there's even a hint of jealousy that it's my mentor who's throwing the party.

But my mind is on when I'm going to do it. When I'm going to tell David that I know. When I will change the course of history, and the course of my future. I keep playing through scenarios, trying to figure out what will happen after I tell him. The telling him, I'm not even worried about. It's what he says next. What if my father scenario is just like Ben's? What if David tells me there was a reason he's shirked his responsibilities for all these years? What if he tells me he hasn't changed his mind, doesn't have any regrets over his decision? That my knowing makes no difference at all to him? What if he tells me he has no interest in having anything to do with me once the Tisch Camp wraps up, and with that, his responsibility as my mentor?

I try to push the thought away, try to channel Dr. Judy, try to remember there's no point in ruminating over what-ifs, but it's futile.

The instructors tell us all we were a pleasure to have in the program and encourage us to keep practicing and that they hope to see us at Tisch next year or the year after that. There are lots of hugs and tears and clinking of plastic glasses filled with ginger ale. And then we file out of the building and make our way to David's. We can hear the music coming from his loft as soon as we enter the building. Ramona skips over to the elevator and presses the button and the doors open and we—Savida, Izzy, Julian, Ben, Ramona and I—pile in, then the boys pull the big door down, and we head up. Savida and Izzy and Julian start dancing to the faint music and then Ramona kisses Julian, whoops and then plants another kiss on Izzy.

"Don't leave a brother hanging," Savida says, pointing at Ben, but Ramona shakes her head. "I don't mow my friends' grass." There's a moment of awkward silence, but then Ramona announces, "Group hug!" and we all wrap our arms around each other.

"This is it. Our last night. When are we all going to be in an elevator again together?" Savida moans, and we all squeeze tighter. Ben on one side of me, Ramona on the other. Sure, there's a chance we all get into Tisch, but Ben, Ramona and Julian would go next year, while Izzy, Savida and I are still juniors, so it's another year off.

"At least you two will still see each other at home." Julian nods at me and Ben.

The elevator bounces as it reaches the fifth floor, and then the boys open the doors and we file out and down the hall. The door to David's studio is open, and the music is near-deafening. There's a DJ in the corner and the place is packed. There has to be at least a hundred people here.

We dump our coats and hats and mitts on the pile at the door.

Stella comes through the door, says hi and walks over to another girl—and I realize it's Talia. Talking to *Gisele Bündchen*. I squeeze Ramona's arm excitedly. "Be cool," she whispers, but how can I be cool when we're at a party that looks like it should be in the pages of *InStyle*?

Someone who looks exactly like Justin Timberlake is DJ'ing in the corner. I snap a discreet pic on my phone and send it to Dace. She's going to die.

David's on the other side of the room, by the couch, and my stomach flips. David. My mentor. My dad? He gives a nod, raises his beer, and I wave back as he takes a swig.

The DJ, upon closer inspection, isn't actually JT. But he's spinning Pharrell Williams and Ramona drags me into the crowd to dance. She throws her head back, singing along, and I do too. "I'm going to miss you!" she yells. "Promise you'll come visit in the summer. And we'll show each other our love on Instagram."

Songs later, Ramona and I take a break to get a drink at the fully stocked makeshift bar in the kitchen. Ben comes up behind me. "So this is it," he says, clinking glasses with us. "I'm gonna go get more ice," Ramona says, making her way to the freezer.

"Can you believe two weeks ago we were total enemies?" I say, taking a sip of my Coke.

He grins. "I hope we're not total enemies now."

I shake my head. "I don't think that's possible. Who would've thought it? Can you believe it's back to boring Spalding tomorrow?"

He shakes his head. "Not for me."

Ramona passes by, flanked by Izzy and Julian. Julian's carrying a bowl of chips and Ramona's got her arm linked through Izzy's. She catches my eye and points over to the couch, where they're heading. I nod but my focus is still on what Ben's just said. I look at him. "What do you mean?"

"I'm not going back." Someone bumps into me, pushing me closer to Ben. He puts a hand out to steady me.

"You're staying the weekend?" I say, but there's something in his voice, in his eyes, that tells me that's not the case.

"Nope. Going to Killington. Dropping out to be a snowboard instructor."

"Um, *what*?" I know I've been wrapped up in my own drama, but this seems like it came out of nowhere.

Lana Del Rey's "West Coast" comes through the speakers. That line about why she's leaving feels strangely coincidental.

"I was always going to do it after high school, but I figure what's the point in finishing? So I can do what? Go to college for the sake of going? When I have absolutely no idea what I want to do with my life after high school? And I don't have any burning desire to go back to Spalding, that's for sure. The school where everyone hates me?"

I look around, trying to process this moment. The lights are dim, the music playing. In the corner, where the couch and chairs are, the mood is mellow. People deep in conversation. Like us.

"But . . . you can't just leave."

"Why not?"

"I'd—I mean . . ." I don't know what I mean. I don't know what I'm trying to say. So I bail on my emotion and stick to facts: "You're going to throw away high school, a diploma, all because you can't wait to be a snowboard instructor?"

He shrugs as Savida passes by, leans in to Ben, says something in his ear. He nods and I feel a stab of . . . what is that? Jealousy? No way. I watch as she walks away, then turn back to face Ben. His blue eyes are fixed on me though.

"Well, have you at least talked to Dr. Judy about this plan?"

"She's going to ask me what I think is the best decision. And I think this is the best decision. They've already got a ton of snow, and they're hiring. It's perfect timing." He shrugs.

"But . . . what about your dad and photography— you're getting good . . ."

"C'mon, Pippa. I'm sucking less. We both know I was never going to make it as a photographer. It was just about my dad. Which in hindsight was so stupid. My mom kept trying to protect me, telling me my dad was just busy. But she knew."

He shoves a hand in his pocket. "You're lucky your dad is dead."

I stare at him, shocked. "It's astounding what a dick thing you just said."

"Shit. That came out wrong." He puts his glass down on the counter. He crosses his arms. He does look miserable. "God, I've been so wrapped up in myself, I didn't even ask you: what—what are you doing about that whole situation? Are you going to tell David that you know?"

The kitchen seems, suddenly, very crowded. "Can we get out of here?" I ask and grab Ben's hand and lead him out to the balcony. There are two heat lamps out there, warming up the cold December air. The Empire State Building's in the distance, the Diamond Hotel too. There are a lot of memories in that skyline.

"If I were David?" Ben says, putting his hands on the railing and leaning over to look down at the street below. He stands back up and faces me. "I would want the chance to get to know you." The wind blows my hair in my face and I turn my face into the wind, to blow it back. He blows in his hands, then rubs them together.

"Pippa, I like you. I like you as more than a friend. I always have. Over the past few months, when you weren't talking to me? It was the worst. And I just kept thinking if I can get to New York, if we can get out of Spalding, out of school, out of the setting where I treated you so wrong, maybe I can

show you I'm different. That I made a mistake—"
He reaches out and pushes away a strand of hair
that's blown back into my face. I don't stop him.

"Sometimes I'd see you in the hallway between
classes, and you wouldn't know I was there, and
you'd be laughing and smiling, with Dace or who-
ever. And I just saw the true you. I'd imagine that
one day that would be me, with you. That you'd be
laughing and smiling because you were hanging out
with me. And this past week . . ."

"Ben, I—"

"I know. And I know it's wrong for me to even be
telling you this. I have no place telling you. Putting
you in this position. And I don't want to put you in
a position. I'm not trying to. I just . . . I know you're
with Dylan, and I can't change that. I had my chance
before you really got together with him, and I know
I screwed up. I was so screwed up. And I have to
live with that. But I can't go back to Spalding. I can't
be there and see you every day and know I can't
be your boyfriend. But I also couldn't leave without
telling you."

Something catches Ben's attention behind me
and I turn around to see. There's a crowd that's
formed around someone who's just come in. I shift
to the left to try to see, but it's just some old guy I
don't recognize. I turn back to Ben, but he's standing,
frozen. He looks strange. He looks astonished.

"That's my dad," Ben says, moving past me,
through the sliding glass doors and into the loft. Ben
goes straight to the group of people. Recognition
flashes in Ben's dad's eyes. He takes a step away

from the crowd, downs the rest of his drink and stretches out his hand to Ben.

And then I turn away. This is Ben's moment with his dad, and it seems almost surreal how quickly things change. How just a moment ago he was out here, telling me . . . telling me he *likes* me? How did this happen? And what do I even think about this? And is the moment gone? Ben's gone, and he's about to get his dad back. Which seems like a sign, that it's my time to go confront David. To tell him that I know he's my dad. To tell him he doesn't have to hide it anymore.

I make my way inside, through the crowd in the studio, to the kitchen, but he's not there, so I head into the hall to the stairwell, to the roof, which has to have at least 50 people on it, drinking and smoking, the rooftop warmed by more heat lamps that glow in the night. I walk around, past a group lying on blankets and pillows, talking, and then three girls sitting together on folding chairs, drinking and laughing. A guy sitting against the wall, texting on his phone. Two guys by the railing, smoking. And then I see him. David's standing with a girl, his hand on her butt, his face buried in the long black waves of her hair. She's wearing a hat—gray and white with a pompom on top. David kisses her—really kisses her. Full tongue. It's not a sight I'd recommend—your parent slipping anyone the tongue. And then the girl changes her position. The light from the heat lamp illuminates her face. Savida.

Repulsion propels me back down into the

stairwell, taking the steps two at a time, and then I'm down the hall, back into David's loft, and through the masses of people drinking, laughing, dancing, back to the balcony, which feels safe. There's a couple at the far end, but otherwise, it's empty. There's the skyline I saw moments ago—New York City all lit up—but it no longer looks magical. It feels vast and I feel lost. I focus on the point where the tip of the tallest buildings meet the dark sky, and I try to process what just happened. Up there, on the roof. I feel sick. Savida? She's *17*. David could be her *father*. And then, well, that thought—David, a father—hits me. I wanted so badly for David to take over the role of being my dad, so that the sadness I feel every day, every hour, of Dad being gone could be gone too. Like a do-over. And I could erase the fact that my dad was dead. Have a fresh start.

Clearly, there's no fresh start to be had. But instead of feeling sorry for myself, I feel ashamed. Ashamed that I was trying to wipe out the 16 years I had with Dad just to eliminate the pain of his death. I think about what Emmy said, how Dad acted *like my dad*, right from the start. David's not a bad person, and he's a good photographer, but a dad? My dad? Somehow, in just a few short minutes, that seems unimaginable, and definitely undesirable.

A guy walks out onto the balcony, and for a minute I think—hope?—it's Ben. It's not, but now I want to find Ben, want to talk to Ben. To tell him what happened. I head back inside, through the throngs, to the couch, where Ramona's still sitting with Izzy and

Julian. She jumps up. "Where have you been?" she asks, hugging me. "I've missed you, roomie!" She's tipsy, and I hug her back, steadying her.

"I know—sorry—but have you seen Ben?"

"He just left." She plops back down on the couch and skooches closer to Izzy, patting the velour beside her, for me to sit. But I stay standing.

"What? He left? Already?"

"He was pretty upset," she says, eating a chip.

"About his dad?"

"His dad?" she looks confused and shakes her head. "No, about *you*."

"Me?"

"Oh god, come on," Ramona says. "The dude can't *stop* talking about you. It would be super annoying if it wasn't you. The guy's in love with you."

I shake my head. "He's not in *love* with me."

Julian pipes up. "Uh, the dude *followed* you to New York. It doesn't get much more romantic than that."

"It's *kind of* pathetic, actually," Izzy says, but Julian reaches over Ramona to smack him on the head. Izzy gives him a dirty look.

"He didn't come here for me," I say, exasperated. "You don't know the whole story. And besides I have a boyfriend."

Ramona nods. "Yeah, yeah. But Ben's leaving. You might never see him again. Just think about that."

"This is too much drama," Julian says, nodding to Izzy. "Let's go harass the DJ." The two of them get up. Julian pats me on the shoulder. Once they're gone, I turn back to Ramona.

"What should I do? What would you do?"

"If I were you . . . I'd go," Ramona says, playing with the silver chain around her neck. "At least to say goodbye." She stands, grabs my hand and starts leading me through the crowd, toward the door. She finds my coat in the heap on the floor, hands it to me and pushes me out the door. I turn back to look at her and she blows me a kiss. "Listen to your gut."

I hurry to the elevator but it's taking forever, so I push open the door to the stairwell, and head down the steps, and out on to the street. It's cold, and I pull my hood up over my head and then grab my phone from my back pocket and text Ben.

Me: Where r u?

No answer. I look in both directions for any sign of a yellow cab. The temperature has dropped, and there's a thin layer of ice on the sidewalk. My ballet flats slip and slide as I pace along the sidewalk, but then I spot a cab. I point at it. "You." And the cab pulls right over to the curb. I open the back door, slide into the backseat and give the address of the dorm to the driver. I check my phone again. Still nothing.

"It's an emergency, so can you go fast? Or, like, as fast as you can without us dying or getting pulled over for speeding?"

"I do my best, ma'am. I do my best." The cabbie steps on it and turns down the next street, past street lamp after street lamp, the city whizzing by. Past Washington Square Park, the fountain lit up in the night sky. A few minutes later, we're pulling in front of the dorm.

I toss a wad of bills at the driver and tumble out of the cab onto the sidewalk, then race inside. "Did you see a guy? With a suitcase?" I pant, breathless, to the security guard. He tilts his head, scratches his chin, like I've got all the time in the world. Then nods. "Yeah," he says, "a few minutes ago."

"Did you see which way his cab went? I think he was going to the airport."

"No cab. He was taking the bus. Asked me which subway to take to get to the Port Authority. Sent him up over to 8th to head uptown."

I run back out onto the street, my feet sliding on the thin layer of ice, and I nearly wipe out several times as I race to 8th Street station. Grab the handrail with my mittens and fly down the steps. I scrabble in my purse for my MetroCard and finally feel the smooth surface, slide it through the reader and push my way through the turnstile onto the platform.

I didn't look at the sign to which track I was on, but there's no way he's still here. I look both ways along the platform, but it's empty. Then I look across to the other side. Ben. Only the train tracks separating us.

"Ben!" I wave, then run down my platform to get across from him and try to catch his attention. "Ben!" I wave wildly just as two trains, one in each direction, rush into the station. I try to peer through the windows of the trains to see if he's seen or heard me, to see if he's still there, but my heart sinks. The doors close and the trains start to move, slowly at first, in opposite directions, until they've fully crossed and exited the station. I drop my head, then dare to look up.

Ben's still there. Suitcase by his side, he's looking straight at me. Waiting.

I take a deep breath, then shout, "Don't go."

ACKNOWLEDGMENTS

They say that writing a book is like having a baby. In this case, it was a race to see what would come first—the final draft of this book or Fitz. Thank you Fitz, for coming early and bringing so much happiness to my life—and then occasionally napping so I could finish the book (even if it required typing with one hand while holding you with the other).

To everyone at ECW, especially Crissy Calhoun, for channeling her inner 16-year-old and making this story a zillion times more believable. Also to Crissy and to Jen Knoch, for basically being Pippa's BFFs and writing things like "<3 <3 <3" and "*Whaaaa?*" in the margins. To Erin Creasey and Jenna Illies, for being so fun to work with. And to everyone else who worked on and supported this book: David Caron, Jack David, Rachel Ironstone, Troy Cunningham, Laura Pastore and Michelle Melski.

Thanks to my first readers and advice-givers: Janis Leblanc and Claudia Grieco for thoughtful insights and edits; Melissa diPasquale for real-life photography notes; Samantha Corbin for taking me into Tischland; and Marissa Stapley for always replying to emails with subject lines like *Hellllllllp* in a split-second. You prove your friendship to me (even though you don't need to!) every single day in so many ways.

My family: Dad, Susan, Danielle, Sarah, Rob, Janet, Terry, Nancy, Ron, Jody, Mark, Cameron, Ally, Julie, Isaac and Levi—for your love, support and much-appreciated babysitting.

Finally, to Penny & Myron for hugs, laughs and caramel sundaes. And to Chris, for insisting we go to New York just *one more time* (research!), for weekend getaways (editing!), dinners out (book meetings!), ping-pong matches (much needed breaks!), chocolate chip cookies (energy to write just one more scene!) and well, everything else. You make me swoon.

CHANTEL GUERTIN is the bestselling author of three novels—*Stuck in Downward Dog, Love Struck* and *The Rule of Thirds*—and a beauty expert on *The Marilyn Denis Show*. When she's not working on a new book, she likes writing in her diary, sending mis-autocorrected texts to her best friends and making to-do lists. She lives in Toronto, Ontario.